VERY RICH

ALSO BY POLLY HORVATH

AN OCCASIONAL COW
(Pictures by Gioia Fiammenghi)

NO MORE CORNFLAKES

THE HAPPY YELLOW CAR

WHEN THE CIRCUS CAME TO TOWN

THE TROLLS

EVERYTHING ON A WAFFLE

THE CANNING SEASON

THE VACATION

THE PEPINS AND THEIR PROBLEMS
(Pictures by Marylin Hafner)

THE CORPS OF THE BARE-BONED PLANE

MY ONE HUNDRED ADVENTURES

NORTHWARD TO THE MOON

MR. AND MRS. BUNNY—DETECTIVES EXTRAORDINAIRE!
(Pictures by Sophie Blackall)

ONE YEAR IN COAL HARBOR

LORD AND LADY BUNNY—ALMOST ROYALTY!
(Pictures by Sophie Blackall)

THE NIGHT GARDEN

VERY RICH

POLLY HORVATH

MARGARET FERGUSON BOOKS
HOLIDAY HOUSE • NEW YORK

Margaret Ferguson Books

Copyright © 2018 by Polly Horvath

All Rights Reserved

HOLIDAY HOUSE is registered in the U.S. Patent and Trademark Office.

Printed and bound in July 2018 at Maple Press, York, PA, USA.

www.holidayhouse.com

First Edition
1 3 5 7 9 10 9 6 4 2

Library of Congress Cataloging-in-Publication Data

Names: Horvath, Polly, author.
Title: Very rich / Polly Horvath.
Description: First edition. | New York : Margaret Ferguson Books,
Holiday House, [2018] | Summary: Ten-year-old Rupert, from a
very large, very poor family, accidently becomes part of an
eccentric rich family's life beginning at Christmas, and
soon sees that wealth is not everything.
Identifiers: LCCN 2017048259 | ISBN 9780823440283 (hardcover)
Subjects: | CYAC: Family life—Ohio—Fiction. | Eccentrics and
eccentricities—Fiction. | Poverty—Fiction. | Wealth—Fiction.
Supernatural—Fiction. | Ohio—Fiction.
Classification: LCC PZ7.H79224 Ver 2018 | DDC [Fic]—dc23
LC record available at https://lccn.loc.gov/2017048259

To Arnie, Emily, Andrew, Zayda, Bonny, and Mildred

CONTENTS

VERY RICH

THE MISTAKE

RUPERT BROWN came from a large family. They lived in a very plain small house on the edge of Steelville, Ohio. Rupert had so many brothers and sisters that it was like living in a small city-state. They crawled over the furniture. They ran in and out of doors. They were big and small and male and female. They all had sandy-brown hair, pinched noses, high cheekbones and narrow lips. They were all thin.

There were so many children in the Brown family that Mrs. Brown claimed not to be able to remember all their names. She often addressed them by "Hey you." Rupert had siblings he rarely talked to and hardly knew. There were many different alliances within the family, many secrets, many separate lives. Close proximity does not always make for coziness. Sometimes it is just crowded.

Rupert was ten, and he moved among his family largely unnoticed except by his favorite sister, six-year-old Elise. She, like Rupert, was quiet and shy and spent a lot of time trying to keep out of everyone's way.

One day before Christmas, Rupert's teenage brothers John and Dirk came home with a cat. Because they were often bringing home stolen cats, there was no doubt in anyone's mind about the origin of this cat. It was not a stray. Perhaps they secretly longed for a pet and this is why they did it, although what they told the family was that it was sport.

"Catch and release. Like fly-fishing. Only with cats," explained John as he held the new one up for his mother to see. There was a wistful look in his eyes. Rupert wondered if he was hoping that his mother would fall in love with it and let them keep it.

"Did I not tell you to stop doing that!" shrieked Mrs. Brown, just home from her job cleaning the offices in the steelworks.

She tore across the room, grabbed the cat, and threw it into the backyard. Then she slammed the door.

Elise looked out the window in concern. "The cat isn't moving," she whispered as Rupert joined her.

"I'll check," Rupert whispered back. Their mother had gone to the kitchen to make the thin gruel of oatmeal that, along with other people's kitchen scraps that their father collected every day, passed for dinner nightly.

All the Brown children tiptoed around their mother. Sometimes she lashed out. Sometimes she hoisted one of the younger Browns onto her lap to watch television and cuddled them as if this, this soft and comforting jolly person, was who she really was. Because you never knew which mother would emerge, it was better to err on the side of caution.

It was cold outside and as Rupert approached the cat he was filled with dread. Suppose the cat was injured? What would they do with it? He knew his mother wouldn't let them keep another mouth that needed feeding. He knew there was no money for a vet. He couldn't just let the cat lie there in pain, could he? Would he himself have to *kill* the cat to put it out of its misery? He didn't know how to do this. What if he had to nurse the cat while keeping his mother at bay? What if the cat was *dead*, then what?

Just as he got close enough to the cat to see that it was still breathing, a cop car came down the road and pulled up in front of the Browns' house. Rupert could see it from where he stood hovering over the cat. The patrol car doors opened and two officers got out and went up the walkway. Oh no, oh no! They were coming for his brothers for sure. If they found the cat would they arrest all three of them, John and Dirk and their mother the cat thrower?

As Rupert reached down, the cat looked up in alarm

and heaved itself to its feet to limp off across the yard. One of its legs must have been hurt in the fall. Rupert ran to the cat, partly to help it and partly with the thought of hiding it from the police. He picked it up and carried it to an empty toolshed in the corner of the yard just as the back door opened and Dirk and John ran through the yard, jumped the fence, and took off across the neighbor's property.

"I'll come back for you later, I promise," Rupert murmured to the cat. Then he went swiftly and silently into the house.

"How dare you!" he heard his mother saying to the police officers at the front door. "Hounding us day and night over cats."

"Mrs. Fraser said she saw your sons very clearly pick up the cat and run away with it," said one of the officers, who looked weary.

"Well, search the place!" cried Mrs. Brown. "Search the darn place from top to bottom then and good luck finding your cat!"

"Are you saying you've let the cat go?" asked the other officer, who also looked weary. Both of the policemen had tired, unhappy cop eyes. The eyes of people who had seen all the sad ways people misbehaved and the terrible things they did to each other but who knew that no matter how tired or sad they became, they must keep knocking on doors to sort things out.

Elise went over to Rupert and took his hand. He squeezed hers. Just then Mr. Brown appeared on the porch with a big bag of kitchen scraps.

"The cops *again?*" He pushed his way between them and into the slightly less chilly clime of the house. "Want a half-eaten taco?" he asked one of the cops with expansive hospitality, rooting through his bag among the carrot greens and almost empty chip bags. "It's here somewhere. It's got most of the meat in it still."

"No, thanks," said the officer, putting up a hand. "I just ate."

"Part of a Twinkie?"

"No, really."

"Here's a bottle of blueberry syrup. I guess they tried it and didn't like it," Mr. Brown said.

"There's a layer of mold on it," said the officer.

Mr. Brown opened the bottle and took a swig. "Tangy!" he reported.

"About your sons, Mrs. Brown," the officer tried again.

Mrs. Brown looked daggers at him. The officers glanced at each other. Their eyes took in everything: the broken-down furniture, the dirty children in their filthy, ragged clothes, the freezing air of the house, Elise and Rupert's frightened faces, the other children who had been one by one creeping up the stairs away from the police and their mother's wrath.

"We'd like to have a brief chat with them, Mrs. Brown," said one of the officers. "They can't keep this behavior up. Everyone knows they steal cats. People are saying they want something done."

"Yeah, and I bet those people all got their cats back," said Mrs. Brown. "People leave their cats to wander the city and poop in other people's yards, but no one arrests the cats or the cat owners for *that*. I say, if you leave your cat to wander the streets, is it any wonder it occasionally goes missing? You people are always picking on the poor. Coming here saying my children are thieves. You never have any proof, have you? Why don't you spend less time picking on innocent people and more time hustling up some real turkeys for the Christmas turkey baskets. *That* would be useful. *That* would be a public service. Every year it's the same. You deliver a basket that you call a Christmas *turkey* basket. But where's the turkey, I'd like to know? A chicken is more like it. And not even a roaster. A fryer."

"Ma'am, they're just *called* Christmas turkey baskets because, well, that's what they've always been called. Some of the baskets have turkeys. Some have chickens. It depends on what's donated. Now where are your sons?"

"How should I know?" asked Mrs. Brown.

"You tell them to watch themselves," said the officer, shrugging and clearly giving up. "Give the cat back to Mrs. Fraser and we'll let it go this time. But if they do it again, we're taking them in."

"Yeah, right, I'll do that," said Mrs. Brown. "If you had any proof, you would have arrested them by now. I wasn't born yesterday." And she slammed the door.

When the car had driven away, Elise whispered to Rupert, "How's the cat?"

"Lame," whispered Rupert before he had a chance to think.

"Lame!" cried Elise.

"What's lame?" barked Mrs. Brown, turning a truly terrible face toward them.

"The cat," whispered Rupert.

"Where?"

"In the toolshed," whispered Rupert, shrinking back to the wall.

"Well, get rid of it!" shrieked Mrs. Brown.

"Your mother's strong as a rock," Mr. Brown said, and then snorted with suppressed glee at his own wit. "You know her secret? She's got no feelings! HAR HAR HAR!" He doubled over with exploding laughter.

"She seems to have anger down pat," muttered Dirk, who was coming through the back door, followed by John.

Mrs. Brown glared at both of them so horribly that Mr. Brown choked back his laugh and turned on the television. Dirk and John joined him on the ramshackle couch and slowly the other children began to drift down the stairs.

Mrs. Brown moved toward the kitchen to sort out the kitchen scraps. As she passed Elise, who was crying quietly over the injured cat and the police visit, she snapped, "Stop that!"

Elise put her thumb in her mouth. She was too old to suck her thumb, but sometimes around her mother it made its way there.

Rupert went out to the toolshed. The cat was lying down licking its front paw. He picked it up and walked the ten blocks to the Frasers' house. It was a harrowing walk, for every moment he expected the cop car to round the corner, see him, and accuse *him* of stealing the cat. He was so worried about this that twice he almost turned around for home, but in the end he feared the police less than he did his mother. Fortunately, he met no one but a man getting off a bus, too focused on scurrying home to wonder what that Brown child was doing with a cat.

When Rupert got to the Frasers' front yard, he gently lowered the cat to the ground, prepared to watch it until it had made its limping way safely to its own door. But the cat had apparently cashed in, if not one of its nine lives, one of its nine recoveries, for whatever limp the cat had had was gone and it ran away from Rupert as quickly as it could.

Rupert found this comforting but worried that the cat would forever after be fearful of people. Perhaps his family had even created a monster who would hiss and scratch anyone who came near. He trudged back home with a heavy heart.

"Is the cat returned?" asked Elise, who was waiting by the front door for him.

"Yes, it's fine and the limp is gone. Go," he whispered fiercely, for his mother had just come out of the kitchen after washing the dinner dishes and was casting an eye about looking for an excuse to yell at someone.

Elise ran up to bed.

"What took you so long?" said his mother. "Dinner is over."

There was never enough food for anyone. They ate quickly when it was ready and without ceremony. Everyone was always hungry. Now, without dinner in his stomach, Rupert felt not just hungry but starving. How long could you starve like this, he wondered as he dragged himself up to bed, before your body began to devour your own bones? He went to sleep and all night dreamt of slithering boneless along the ground.

The next morning Rupert waited in front of the school for Elise, who always walked there a little later than Rupert, who liked to be early. When she approached he went up to her and said, "We could try lining up for the free breakfast again."

"I'm too scared," said Elise.

"Yeah, me too," said Rupert, and went to lean by the entrance until the bell rang. Elise ran off to her classroom in a different wing.

There was a free breakfast program for hungry children, but he never got to partake of it because the lunch lady who served it didn't like the Browns either. John and Dirk had stolen her cat and it took three days for it to return to her. She never forgave them. As far as she was concerned, all the Browns were tarred with the same larcenous brush. The one time Rupert showed up in line for his free breakfast she gave him such a look that he was shaken to his core and never returned. Neither did his brothers or sisters.

Because Rupert was so thin he should have felt as if he were bursting with health. Doctors now tell you very thin is a healthy state to be in. The healthiest state, really. If you ask them, they will tell you that it would do all of us some good to fast a couple of days a week. It kills off your bad cells so your good cells can flourish. But Rupert, thin as he was, fairly bursting with good cells and no room in his body for the bad ones, didn't feel healthy. Every day he walked home from school, desperately trying to make it to his own porch before the dizziness of hunger overcame him. And every day when he got there he felt like he might faint right on his doorstep.

Once he got home, he would go to his bedroom. There were three bedrooms in the house. One for the boys, one for the girls, and one for Mr. and Mrs. Brown. In the boys' and girls' bedrooms, the younger children slept in the beds and the older ones slept under them. Rupert shared the underneath of a bed with John and Dirk. After school Rupert often lay under the boys' bed garnering his energy so he would have enough to drag himself downstairs when the dinner oatmeal was ready. Then the oatmeal gave him just enough energy to crawl back upstairs and fall asleep. This was his life. A life spent hoping he wouldn't disgrace himself by fainting.

Then one day it happened. He did faint. It happened on a day of very deep snow.

Rupert got up and left for school as usual. In order to get there, he would start out from his house in the very poor people's area on the outskirts of town by the railroad tracks and power station. Houses there were derelict. Then he would pass through the poor but proud part where people with little money made a decent effort to keep their lawns tidy and their steps swept. Next, he came to the middle-class houses, brimming with hedges and gardens and tidy shutters framing what Rupert imagined were only happy, well-fed people, then to the more opulent houses of the rich. And finally, before he got to the school, he trekked past the houses of the very rich.

As he set out, Rupert thought it odd that his mother hadn't made the sparse spoonful-per-person morning oatmeal that morning. And odd that no one had made any tracks before him on the sidewalk. He had to step high and cut through the deep drifts of heavy, wet snow. This was especially taxing as he had no boots, only tennis shoes, but he didn't dare walk in the road. They were never plowed properly and cars were always dovetailing on their slick surfaces. A boy was too apt to be run over there, although this day there seemed to be little traffic and that was yet another odd thing.

Rupert considered giving up and missing school, but he wanted to grow up to do something special. He wasn't sure what yet, but he knew you couldn't do any kind of special thing without school. So he forced himself to trudge forward. *Mind over matter*, he chanted to himself, *mind over matter*. At one point, he sat down and a drift of snow collapsed over him. The wet snow turned his neck red because he had no scarf or hat. He had no coat either. He had to make do by wearing all three shirts he owned, one on top of the other, and a hole-ridden sweatshirt over all. This worked okay until the dead of winter. Then he was not only always hungry, he was always cold. He was nearly frostbitten when he stood up again. So much so, he wasn't sure he could go on. But the happy thought that any moment he would be inside the heated school kept him going. It was just around the next corner.

Yet when he rounded the corner there were no cars, no children racing about throwing snowballs, no lights, no buses. There was only what appeared to be an empty building. He stared in dismay.

Rupert knew he must have gotten something wrong.

Either this is the weekend, he said to himself, *or it is a professional development day or a holiday.* Mornings were such a blur for him, always tired, always hungry, that except for the absence of the oatmeal, he hadn't even noticed that his family wasn't up preparing for the day. Well, there was nothing for it. He would have to turn around and go home. He would have to try not to faint or freeze to death. *Mind over matter,* he said to himself again, *mind over matter.* At least he had his own tracks to walk back in. He wouldn't have to break the virgin snow with his tennis shoes. It would save a little energy. At least he had *that*. He began the walk home.

First he passed through the very rich people's enclave. There were seven mansions here. All on huge lots with high fences or hedges and gates that defied even the John and Dirk cat stealers of the world. The very rich people were not just safe themselves, their cats were safe.

Rupert was walking in front of one of these gates when it swung open to allow a departing car to pass through. The gate swung right into Rupert. A curly decorative piece of iron hooked into one of the holes of his sweatshirt and hoisted him up. This was when Rupert fainted. The gate continued opening, causing his unconscious hanging body to bounce against its iron rails. *Bang, bang, bang.*

Rupert was just waking up from his faint with the thought that on top of everything else he was probably going to bruise when the car pulled through the gate and stopped. A woman stuck her head out the window and stared at him.

She said, "Is that a body swinging from the gate, Billingston?"

"I do believe you're right, Mrs. Cook," said Billingston, who was driving.

"Well, use the electric charge button. That's what it's there for. To deter gate-crashers."

The next thing that happened was a huge jolt of electrical current passed through Rupert's little shop-worn body and caused him to buck and bang hard against the metal gate again. The gate began to close and the car drove on, Mrs. Cook satisfied that this would be the end of such high jinx. Billingston, as he drove away, pressed the gate charge button one more time for good measure. This one jolted Rupert into the air and he ended up flying right over the top of the seven-foot hedge and landing on the wrong side of it. That is, on the *mansion* side. On the snowy lawn of these very rich people. Exactly where no one really wanted him to be. Rupert expected to feel at any second the thick, viscous drool of vicious guard dogs, followed by their sharp, ripping teeth. He had come to find that the worst thing that you anticipated, the worst thing you could even *imagine*, was usually what happened. So he waited patiently to be consumed. He hadn't even the energy to move, let alone fight them off. Whole minutes passed. But no dogs came bounding up to him. No cats either. Clearly these were not animal people.

Rupert started to get up when he heard a voice say, "How did *you* get here?"

It was Turgid Rivers. The richest boy at school. He was in the sixth grade, a grade above Rupert.

"I guess you must live here," said Rupert weakly.

Turgid nodded.

"Nice house," said Rupert.

And then he fainted again.

A DINNER INVITATION

THIS TIME when Rupert woke up he was lying in front of a big, warm fireplace. There was Turgid's small, curious face hanging above, staring at him.

At first he thought he must be in the Riverses' living room—the carpet was so thick and luxurious, the fireplace so large, and the fire in it so roaring—but gradually as he gained full consciousness and began to turn his head this way and that, he realized he was in a bedroom. From the look of the toys, Turgid's bedroom.

"My goodness," said Turgid, "Christmas is always very exciting. You never know what you're going to find. But I didn't expect to find a dead schoolmate on my front lawn. I dragged you in here. You're not very heavy."

"I'm not dead," said Rupert.

"Well, you're not very lively! How did you get past the gate?" asked Turgid.

"As far as I can tell, I got jolted over it by an electric shock," said Rupert.

"Oh, the security system. But why aren't you at home with your family? It's Christmas morning."

"Is it?" asked Rupert.

"Yes, of course. You must know that, surely," said Turgid.

"That explains why no one was at school," said Rupert feebly. He really felt quite ill. Between the starvation and the cold and the electric shocks, he was not at his best.

"You actually went to school?" asked Turgid in amazement. "But wasn't waking up to a stocking full of toys some kind of clue?"

"We don't do that. I think I'm going to faint again," said Rupert sickly.

"Goodness," said Turgid. "Anything I can do to help? Why do you keep fainting like this? It can't be normal. Are you ill?"

"I think it's the hunger," said Rupert. "But it might be the cold. It's not the electric jolts, because I felt this way before that happened, so you mustn't blame yourselves."

"Oh, no fear, we never blame ourselves around *here*. Well, gosh, what can we do for you? Have some chocolate!" And Turgid grabbed a large chocolate Santa from a pile of trinkets by his bed. "I got it in my stocking."

"Are you sure?" asked Rupert. "It's *your* Christmas chocolate."

"Well, I don't want you fainting all over the house," said Turgid.

He broke off a chocolate arm and gave it to Rupert, who sat up and crammed it into his mouth. He immediately felt better. He could feel the chocolate ooze all over his tongue and run down into his stomach, where it awoke a hunger so vast, it was as if the chocolate were a flame thawing Rupert's frozen insides and igniting the appetite therein.

"More," croaked Rupert through a mouthful of chocolate and drool.

Turgid gave him the whole Santa and looked politely away. Rupert was a mess.

When Rupert had consumed the Santa and three chocolate Christmas ornaments that Turgid gave him for good measure, he felt much better. That was when he noticed he was wet through and, despite the roaring fire, was shivering madly.

"You need dry clothes," said Turgid.

He ran to his closet and got the warmest things he could find: sweatpants and a sweatshirt and socks, all fleece. Then he ran to his bathroom to get a towel for Rupert's drool while Rupert changed.

Rupert was warm and dry and while not full, not fainting from starvation either.

"Thank you. Thank you," was all he could say.

"Never mind," said Turgid. "This is rather fun. It's like having a pet."

"But I have to get home," said Rupert. If this really was Christmas, it was the day they got their Christmas turkey basket. It was only once a year. He didn't want to miss it.

"Oh no," said Turgid. "You must have Christmas dinner with us. I insist. It may not be our fault, but as a consequence of our security system you've had a terrible shock. It must have been Mrs. Cook who gave the order to shock you. She's our cook. The name is purely coincidental. We don't for instance call our butler Mr. Butler. His name is Billingston and he's probably the one who actually pressed the button. Although I'm sure it was on Mrs. Cook's orders. Mrs. Cook is a little too fond of watching people frizzle up from electric jolts. She was leaving to get a Christmas goose because Aunt Hazelnut said it wouldn't be Christmas without a goose. Mrs. Cook had planned on prime rib. We've never had a goose, but Aunt Hazelnut has been reading a lot of Dickens because the librarian living here keeps bringing it home for her—"

"You have your own librarian?" interrupted Rupert in amazement. Oh, these rich people!

"Yes, but it's not what you think. We don't employ her. We're not even quite sure who she is. Well, I mean, Uncle Moffat should know. What happened was, he made the mistake of offering one of our bedrooms as a raffle prize in a fundraiser. I think he meant for someone to come and just spend the weekend. People are always wanting to know what it's like in the Rivers mansion. This librarian won and moved in with a suitcase and never moved out. We all started politely ignoring her, which is what Uncle Moffat said we should do to whoever won. For their sake as much as ours. You know, let them observe us freely without making them uncomfortable. But instead of going back home Monday she just stayed on and on and we kept ignoring her and she kept spying on us from behind chairs and curtains and such and in the end we simply all got used to the arrangement. I wouldn't say we like it exactly, but she makes herself useful. She brings home books if you let her. Anyhow, I guess they're always chowing down on goose in Dickens, so off Aunt Hazelnut sent Mrs. Cook for one. Mrs. Cook was in quite a temper. She hates last-minute menu changes. So that's probably why she shocked you. It wasn't personal. She was in a mood. That and her enjoyment of the 'moment of frizzle' as she puts it. So you see, you must have dinner with us. Should I phone your family to let them know?"

"We haven't a phone," said Rupert.

"How odd," said Turgid. "Are you odd people?"

Rupert didn't know how to answer this. He wanted to say no, they were ordinary. Or ordinaryish. They simply couldn't *afford* a phone. However, to say this would be to expose his extreme poverty, which was embarrassing. So he said nothing. Also, he thought, perhaps to a rich person being poor *is* odd.

When Rupert didn't answer, Turgid said, "Well, shall I send Billingston to your house to inform your family?"

"That's all right. They won't care," said Rupert before he had time to think.

"Won't care if you miss your own Christmas dinner?" asked Turgid.

Rupert thought if they did notice he was missing, which was unlikely, they would simply be glad there was one less person to fight over the paltry amount of chicken. Except for Elise. She would probably notice he was missing, but even she would most likely be too focused on getting some chicken to be worried. This is what extreme hunger did to people.

"No, we're very casual about those things," said Rupert, knowing he couldn't possibly explain the complications of a life so different from Turgid's own.

"Well, then it's settled."

Someone shouted from downstairs for Turgid. He pulled Rupert with him to the top of the stairs.

"Turgid, darling!" called the voice again from some

recess of the house. "Mrs. Cook couldn't find a goose at the only store open on Christmas, so it's prime rib after all. Everything is ready. Mrs. Cook wants us to eat so she can get out of here. She wants dinner with her own family."

"All right, Mother," Turgid called back. "It's a little early, isn't it?"

It was ten in the morning.

"She's been up cooking since four apparently," Mrs. Rivers's disembodied voice went on. "Come on, let's indulge her. It's Christmas, after all. Aren't you hungry?"

"Not terribly. I've been eating chocolates all morning. Are you hungry, Rupert?" asked Turgid.

"I'm always hungry," said Rupert truthfully.

"Rupert is starving!" called Turgid. "He's having dinner with us. That's all right, isn't it, Mother?"

"Oh good," said Mrs. Rivers. "Someone else for the games. The games are always better with more people."

THE GAMES

A FEW minutes later everyone converged in the dining room.

"Well," said Uncle Moffat as they all sat down, "it seems every year we eat at a more ridiculous time."

"Yes, what's with such an early dinner?" asked Turgid's little sister, Sippy.

"Are we having an early dinner or are we having roast beef for breakfast, that's the question," said Uncle Henry. He was a thin man with a beak of a nose and a mass of unruly white hair.

"Should I tell you who all these people are?" Turgid asked Rupert as Billingston set an extra place for him.

"I'll never remember them all," said Rupert, thinking, *Get to the food, get to the food.*

"Oh, sure you will. That's my brother, Rollin, my sister, Sippy. My mother is the stocky one sitting next to you at the head of the table with the blond hair and the weird glasses that make her eyes look like they're squinting,"

he said quietly so she didn't hear. "That's my father heading up the other end of the table. There's my Uncle Moffat - he's the fat one with the bright red cheeks. He lives
here with my cousins, who are all awful. Their names are
William, Melanie, and Turgid. You don't have to worry
about talking to them. They usually spend the whole of
dinner arguing among themselves. Their mother, Aunt
Anne, has left to dairy farm in Wisconsin—don't ask.
My Uncle Henry is in the purple smoking jacket sitting
in front of the fireplace. My Aunt Hazelnut is the stringy,
very white powdery lady with the curly red hair next to
him. She's easy to remember because she's the only other
woman here who isn't my mother."

"Did you say another Turgid? Is it a family name?"

"No, and there was a huge fight about it when Uncle
Moffat and Aunt Anne announced they were naming
their son Turgid too. Oh, and that's the librarian that
I mentioned earlier, spying at us from behind the curtains. I forgot there was another woman here besides
Mother and Aunt Hazelnut. I always forget about her
at dinners because she doesn't say a lot. We don't know
much about her past and don't feel we are familiar
enough to ask. But you can ask her anything else. She
knows everything. Just try it. Go ahead, try it. Mother
thinks she must be a reference librarian."

"Maybe later," said Rupert.

He was feeling shy and overwhelmed. Everyone

was talking at once now and the cacophony filled the room. Mrs. Cook had come in with a tureen and was ladling soup into bowls from the head of the table and Billingston was placing them before people.

As the soup reached the other Turgid, he picked up his spoon and began eating when Uncle Henry cried out, "THE CRACKERS!"

"Put your spoon down, Turgid," said Aunt Hazelnut.

"Oh, I hate the crackers," said Mr. Rivers. "What a load of nonsense."

"Nonsense? Everyone loves the crackers," said Uncle Henry, holding up what appeared to Rupert to be a gift-wrapped cylinder with ruffled ends.

He watched at first before trying it with Turgid, as each person took turns pulling on an end of his own cracker and the one belonging to the person next to him. Little explosions occurred, and then the cylinders were ripped open and a paper crown, a joke, and a party favor poured out of each one.

"Everyone, read your joke out loud before we eat," commanded Uncle Henry.

"What did one snowman say to the other?" called out Sippy.

"Do you smell carrot?" screamed Aunt Hazelnut, shrieking with laughter.

"What did one reindeer say to the other?" read Uncle Henry.

"I don't know," said Uncle Moffat.

"Nothing. Reindeer can't talk," read Uncle Henry.

Around the table they went. When it was Rupert's turn, he nervously began to unfold the bit of paper with his joke when Uncle Henry said, "Wait a second. Who are *you*?"

"R-R-R-Rupert," stammered Rupert.

"Well, that doesn't tell us much," said Uncle Moffat.

"He was found on our front lawn, half frozen and fainted dead away," said Turgid.

"Goodness, another librarian?" asked Uncle Henry.

"Don't be ridiculous!" roared Uncle Moffat. "He can't be more than nine years old."

"Ten, almost eleven," corrected Rupert in a whisper.

"People do seem to be just showing up and moving in of late," said Mr. Rivers, who never had been apprised of the circumstances surrounding the librarian. He worked long hours and was often out of the loop, family-news-wise.

"What's wrong with his speaking voice?" asked William.

"Nothing at all, shut up and read your joke," said Turgid.

"He could be a librarian-in-training," said Uncle Henry, ignoring them all. "That would account for the whispering. They are always telling people in libraries to whisper. I bet I'm right! I'm sure I'm right. Am I right, boy?"

"No," whispered Rupert.

"HA!" said Uncle Moffat.

"I hope you've unfrozen," said Mrs. Rivers kindly.

"Yes, thank you," whispered Rupert.

"Wait a second!" screamed Mrs. Cook, who was bringing in olives and celery. "Are you the kid I tried to jolt off the gate?"

"It wasn't my fault," explained Rupert frantically. "I was walking by and the gate snagged a hole in my sweatshirt."

"Oh, Mrs. Cook, not the frizzle again?" said Mrs. Rivers reprovingly.

"I keep telling you people," said Mrs. Cook, "I don't like watching people frizzle up any more than most. I'm just deterring burglars. I ought to get paid extra."

"Come, you like to see them frizzle up a *bit*, admit it," said Uncle Henry.

"Oh a *bit*, everyone likes to see people frizzle up a *bit*," said Mrs. Cook defensively.

"I don't see any holes in your sweatshirt now, young man," said Mr. Rivers, craning his neck forward over his soup bowl to peer at Rupert.

"He's wearing my sweatshirt, Father," said Turgid. "Will everybody please leave him alone? Rupert, read your joke."

"What did one reindeer say to the other?" read Rupert.

"We've already *had* that one!" called out Uncle Moffat accusingly.

"There's always a few repeats, you know that," said Uncle Henry. "Enough. We're done with the crackers. Everyone eat your soup."

And just like that everyone did. Rupert noticed they were now all wearing the paper crowns from their crackers, so he put his own crown on and began to eat as well. The soup was the most delicious thing Rupert had ever eaten. It was full of cream and potato and he knew not what else. He ate it in quick, quiet spoonfuls and finished before everyone else. He wished he could have more, but as soon as he was done Billingston swept his bowl away.

While Rupert waited for the others to finish, he looked at his party favor. It was a small plastic-wrapped deck of cards.

"What am I supposed to do with this?" he whispered to Turgid, although he need not have whispered because now everyone was eating and talking and drinking wine (the adults) and Shirley Temples (the children) and the room was full of happy festive noise.

"I dunno," said Turgid.

"Well, what are you doing with your favor? What *is* yours?"

"Hmmm, looks like a key chain," said Turgid. "We usually keep them around with the general clutter and mess of Christmas and then I don't know where they disappear to. Get thrown out, I suspect. Nobody really wants the things they get in the Christmas crackers. It's the same boring, worthless junk year to year. But, you know, you have to put up with it because, well, it's part of Christmas, isn't it? Doesn't your family do Christmas crackers?"

Rupert wanted to say, my family doesn't even do food, which wasn't quite true because of the Christmas turkey baskets. Although there was never enough chicken to go around, everyone got something from the basket. The rest of the food in the basket came from the food bank and it was mostly things people had found in their cupboards and regretted buying and so ended up putting in the food bank bins. It was heavy on the smoked octopus and chipotle-chickpeas kind of groceries, which, heaven knows, the Browns didn't object to. They were more than happy to eat Steelville's grocery mistakes.

"No, we've never done Christmas crackers," said Rupert.

If Turgid couldn't figure out that a person who couldn't afford winter boots or a coat probably couldn't afford Christmas crackers, Rupert wasn't going to appear unfriendly by pointing it out. Rupert wasn't even sure that Turgid had *noticed* his lack of boots and coat. He started to hide the small deck of cards under his bread plate when he realized that there was a roll sitting on it. He ate the roll and then saw the butter pat and he stuck

that whole into his mouth and let it melt in savory wonder all over his tongue. He'd never had butter. The only
kind of fat the Browns ever saw was lard. He liked lard
but the butter was simply out of this world. And all the
time he was thinking that if the Riverses were throwing
out the party favors perhaps it would be okay if he kept
his. In fact, maybe he could somehow scoop up all the
party favors before they got thrown out and take them
home. He had never had a toy before and neither had his
brothers or sisters. So he slowly palmed the cards and
slid his hand to the edge of the table and then down to
his side. He put the cards in the pocket of Turgid's sweatpants, to be transferred later to his own pants.

When he looked up from this covert operation he
found Uncle Henry eyeing him thoughtfully. Rupert
blushed. He blushed until he thought he must be the
color of an eggplant. He blushed until he thought he
would explode. He quickly looked at his plate, but
when he finally lifted his eyes again he saw that Uncle
Henry had wiped the thoughtful expression off his face.
He winked at Rupert and turned to talk to Sippy.

Being caught out was terrible. He was sure he had just
done what they all expected a poor boy from the wrong
side of town to do and he was filled with embarrassed
regret, but at that moment the rest of the soup bowls were
carried out of the room and Mrs. Cook began to bring
in such a variety of tureens and platters that Rupert's

embarrassment was supplanted by excitement. He had never seen or smelled such food in his life. It would have been an extraordinary dinner for someone who ate well, but for someone living on thin oatmeal and kitchen scraps, it was a sight not to be believed. There was roast beef and mashed potatoes and roasted potatoes and Yorkshire pudding and gravy and biscuits and carrots and corn and beans and stuffing. There was cranberry sauce and cloudberry jelly and sour pickles and sweet pickles and hot pickles and chocolate pickles. There was cheese soufflé and spinach soufflé and spoonbread. There were so many kinds of food, so much food, and it began to be passed around the table at such speed that before he knew it, Rupert had a meal mountain before him on his plate.

He sat silently through the rest of dinner, eating away with intense concentration, feeling like a bear about to go into hibernation. He must put on all the weight he needed for winter. This is for January, he thought, taking more potatoes. This is for February, he thought, loading his plate up again with prime rib and pouring gravy on top.

By now he was feeling a little unwell, but just as he finished his last bite his plate was taken away and the pies were brought in: mince and apple and pumpkin and cherry and chocolate and banana. There were cookies and custards, éclairs and cake. There was pudding. There was fruit. There was cheese.

But Rupert knew with sick disappointment that he could not eat a bite of any of it. He was full to the top. He could literally feel the food pressing on the top of his esophagus and threatening to make its way back into his mouth. There was no room, not a hairbreadth of space for more.

"Oh, you must have some dessert, Rupert," said Mrs. Rivers after a bit, noticing how, unlike the family, engaged in a general free-for-all among the sweets, he was not reaching for any of it.

"I can't," said Rupert.

"You shouldn't have stuffed so during dinner," said Melanie through a mouth full of pie. "I saw you."

"You shut up," said Turgid.

"I'm just saying," said Melanie.

"Rupert can have his dessert later after the games when everyone else is having their seconds and thirds," said Mrs. Rivers. "I'm not hungry anymore myself. Billingston, take it all away."

So Billington took away all the plates with their half-eaten pies and cookies and custards. Away went all the cracker wrappers and jokes and favors. He collected the crowns, which Rupert relinquished regretfully. He had been hoping to save his for Elise, but it was tossed into the fire with the rest. Nothing remained on the table except everyone's drinking glasses.

For the first time Rupert noticed his untouched

Shirley Temple. He was very thirsty. He had just enough room now for a sip. It was delicious. It was red and bubbly and topped with a maraschino cherry. Like everything else he'd had today it was the best drink, the most wondrous *version* of a drink he'd ever had. He was so delighted he felt like crying. But he had no time because now Billington was bringing in a pile of wrapped prizes and spreading them all over the table.

Mrs. Cook came into the dining room to say good-bye. She had on her coat and hat and gloves and was departing finally for home to have Christmas with her family.

"Oh, Mrs. Cook," said Mrs. Rivers, "your presents are on the buffet."

"Thank you," said Mrs. Cook frostily. Every year she thought the Riverses took too long at dinner. She felt sure they did this to spite her. She had a large shopping bag and two garbage bags with her. She opened them up and scooped the dozens of presents from the Rivers family into them.

"We hope you find something there you like," said Mrs. Rivers, and, turning to Rupert, whispered, "She never much likes what we get her. Oh well."

Rupert didn't know what to say back. Mrs. Rivers seemed to like him, and this was an unusual occurrence for Rupert. It wasn't that people disliked him for himself. Some disliked him for his position in life,

his general dishevelment and, he feared, his smell—
although he tried to bathe as often as he could get bathroom time in that crowded house—and others disliked
him for his brothers' cat stealing. That pretty much
covered all the people in town, so he was not accus-
tomed to being thought well of.

Mrs. Cook marched ceremoniously out of the dining
room, dragging her bags behind her.

"Oh, and Mrs. Cook," called Mrs. Rivers, "if you
should find anyone swinging from the gate, let's give
them a pass? It being Christmas and all."

Mrs. Cook didn't stop or turn back, but she nodded
and left.

"All right," said Uncle Moffat, rubbing his hands in
glee. "Pass the Parcel first?"

"I don't know how to play," Rupert whispered to
Turgid.

"Oh, it's easy," said Turgid. "Everyone picks a
folded piece of paper with a number on it from a hat we
pass around. The person who has the number one picks
a prize from the table and unwraps it. Then number two
does the same, but number two can now decide whether
to keep his prize or exchange it for number one's. Then
number three, when it is his turn, can decide to keep his
prize or exchange it for number one's or number two's.
Once your turn is past, you have no chance for selection. The best number to draw is obviously the last, as

that person has the choice of exchanging his prize for anything anyone else has. Some prizes are quite good and others are awful."

"The goal is to make a number of people very unhappy," Uncle Henry joined in. "Inevitably someone breaks down and cries."

"Oh no," said Rupert.

"That's the best part, my boy!" said Uncle Henry. "Spare no one's feelings. If they have something they particularly want, trade for it when it's your turn. Take it away from them. Make them miserable. That's the entertainment factor of this game in a nutshell."

Rupert had no plans to do this. He figured he would be fine with anything he won. He had gotten through life so far by being unobtrusive and not making waves or enemies.

Billingston brought in the hat with the bits of folded-up paper. It was passed around the table. Rupert picked one and opened it. He got the number four.

"That's not the best number," said Melanie knowingly.

"Or the worst," said the other Turgid.

When everyone had a number before him, Mrs. Rivers, who had picked number one, chose and unwrapped a prize first. It was an orange.

"Oh, well, I guess I'm stuck," she said morosely. "No one will ask me to trade. Why do I always get a low number? In all the years I have been playing this game why have I *never* gotten a good number? I think it's fixed."

"You say that every year," said Mr. Rivers, who had picked number two. He got a set of Nancy Drew books.

"Splendid," he said. "I've never read these. I can see a very pleasant week ahead of me."

"*If* you get to keep them," chimed in William.

"Which you won't," said Melanie determinedly. She had number three and was busy unwrapping her prize. It was a box of chocolates. "Right. I'll just trade these for your set of Nancy Drew books, thank you," and she ran around the table to Mr. Rivers's place to snatch them. She tossed him her chocolates.

"And I don't even like chocolate," said Mr. Rivers sadly.

"Perhaps you'd prefer an orange?" asked Mrs. Rivers.

"You wish," said Mr. Rivers, and stared sulkily out the window.

"I like chocolate," said Sippy hopefully.

"You can't exchange now," barked Uncle Henry. "You've both had your turn. And you certainly can't give the chocolate away to Sippy; she knows very well that's completely against the rules! You're stuck with your lot. No cheating!"

Now it was Rupert's turn. He picked a small prize and opened it. It was a kazoo.

"Oh, thank you," he whispered. He had no idea what it was.

"Who are you thanking?" scoffed William.

"That's a rotten prize," said the other Turgid.

"Yeah, it is, but you can't have my Nancy Drew books," said Melanie threateningly. "So don't even think about it."

"He can have anything he wants!" said Uncle Henry.

"He doesn't even *live* here," complained Melanie.

"That's not a rule," said Uncle Henry. "If you want to institute a new rule you must apply to the rules commission. You can't just come up with a new rule such as one must live here to get the good prizes."

"There is no rule commission," said Melanie. "You're making that up."

"Of course there's a rule commission," said Uncle Henry. "How could we have a set of rules otherwise? Are you stupider than a paramecium? Are you completely insensate?"

"Oh dear," said Mrs. Rivers. "Now you've made her cry."

"I was just asking the important questions," said Uncle Henry. "Questions she should be asking herself."

"Am I stupider than a paramecium?" shouted Melanie, standing up. "I don't even know what a paramecium *is*!"

"I rest my case," said Uncle Henry, folding his hands and nodding quietly.

"And I'm not crying!" Melanie continued to shout. "Uncle Henry makes up the rules as he goes along and then makes up institutions to cover for it!"

"I don't! I never did!" said Uncle Henry, rising in indignation and coming eye to eye with Melanie.

"Take her books, boy," said Uncle Moffat to Rupert. "That'll teach her."

"I think I'll just keep this thing, thank you," whispered Rupert, clutching his kazoo.

"You don't even know what it is!" said the other Turgid, crowing with laughter.

"He doesn't play in the spirit of the game!" said Rollin.

"Right," said William. "He's no fun."

"You shut up," said Melanie. "Of course he wants a kazoo. Who wouldn't?"

"My turn," said Turgid, changing the subject by opening his small prize.

It was the new 1996 Farmer's Almanac. He traded it for his father's chocolates. He would have taken the Nancy Drew books but he was afraid of Melanie.

"Thank God," said Mr. Rivers, looking at the Almanac for the new year. "At least this is useful." And he started reading the weather prediction for January.

"Wouldn't you really rather have an orange, Turgid dear?" asked his mother.

"You know I wouldn't," said Turgid.

"I don't know why we keep oranges in the house," said Mrs. Rivers glumly. "Nobody likes them."

"I like them, I would just prefer the box of chocolates," said Turgid.

"But I gave birth to you," Mrs. Rivers said.

"Let's not start that again," said Turgid.

Mrs. Rivers tended to bring this up whenever things didn't go her way.

"Thirteen hours of excruciating labor," Mrs. Rivers droned on to herself. No one else paid the least attention.

"You know an orange or a banana used to be considered an exotic item, a luxury item," said the librarian from behind the curtains. She had spent dinner helping herself to little plates of food from the table and going back to her seat behind the curtains, picking at her meal while alternately reading and eavesdropping. "At one time children would have been filled with excitement to get such a food item."

"Thank you for sharing," said Uncle Moffat, rolling his eyes slightly.

"And welcome to the twentieth century and the age of modern refrigeration," said Mr. Rivers. "Can we just keep this game going, please?"

And on it went until William unwrapped a small dead mouse and traded it for Melanie's set of Nancy

Drew books, which caused her to cry miserably and wail that she hated this family.

"Ha ha, Melanie got the booby prize," sang William.

"Billingston is in charge of the prizes and every year, by Jove, he tops himself with a horrible booby prize!" crowed Uncle Henry. "Last year it was a piece of moldy cheese. Well, Melanie, my dear, looks like you're stuck with a dead mouse. How quickly our circumstances change in life. *Whoosh whoosh* on top of the world and then *whoosh whoosh* not. No one is going to trade for *that*. And anyway, now the game's over."

"Oh, Melanie, please don't take on so, you can get the books out of the library," said the librarian through the curtains. "I've always told you, with a library card you can never be poor."

"She's never going to be poor anyway," said Mr. Rivers. "She's a Rivers."

But Melanie was too busy wailing to hear anyone else. As far as they could tell, it was something rather incoherent about just wanting to win.

Finally Aunt Hazelnut said, "Oh, do shut up, Melanie, it's just a game."

And Uncle Henry stood up and cried, "NEXT!"

And they proceeded. For the more physical games they moved to the living room.

Charades was played. Statues was played. Scattergories, Pictionary, and Dictionary were played. Meanwhile, more and more prizes were brought out by Billingston from a seemingly endless store. Rupert had amassed a mountain of them. And *what* prizes. He had a train set and warm winter boots. They were two sizes too big for him but he didn't care. He had a snow shovel and a membership in the Cookie of the Month Club. He had a radio activated plane. He had a pile of warm sweaters. And the best part, he thought, was for the first time he could give his family Christmas presents. The only other presents the Browns had ever received were given by John and Dirk and tended to be largely—well, entirely—cats.

Rupert sat happily thinking who would get what. One of his younger brothers would get the train set. His father could have the radio-activated plane. He was sure he would love it. It would be something to do while he watched television. The sweaters could be divided among all of them. Some of them were even large enough to fit his mother. There was a stuffed tiger and a stuffed lion for John and Dirk. As teenagers they were perhaps too old for stuffed animals but Rupert hoped they might find them suitable substitutes for live cats. And he now possessed the set of Nancy Drew books which William had lost again to Melanie in a game called Pick and which Melanie had then been forced to surrender to Rupert in a game Uncle Henry had made up and which was his favorite, calling it Forfeit, in which everyone's favorite prize could be lost.

Rupert was afraid of Melanie ever since he had won the books, but Uncle Henry had assured him that Melanie was always frightening during the games, that it was good for her to learn sportsmanship, and that he should ignore her. The books, if Melanie didn't exact revenge, would go to his sister Elise. Elise liked to sit with Rupert in the evening and Rupert tried to make up stories to tell her to keep their minds off the cold. But they were never very good stories. He had experienced little in life so far except hunger and cold, so those tended to creep into the stories, making them somewhat useless as a distraction. But now he could read her all the Nancy Drew books. This made him happier than anything that had occurred that day.

Finally, in the middle of the afternoon, the Rivers came to their last game.

ONE LAST QUESTION

ALL RIGHT, everyone," called Uncle Henry. "Bring all your prizes back to the dining room table."

"Are these really mine?" Rupert whispered to Turgid, pointing to the mountain of prizes he was lugging. There were too many to place on the table and he had to pile a bunch of them up behind his chair as well.

"They're yours, all right," said Turgid. "You won them fair and square. Not bad for your first games."

Rupert could hardly believe it. None of this was what he had come to expect from life. He could hardly believe his luck in getting snagged by the terrible gate and jolted over it. *It just goes to show*, he thought, *that you mustn't be too hasty to judge the events in your life: what is good or bad or may lead to better or worse things.* He thought he knew what to expect, but it turned out you never do know.

He didn't realize it, but in his delight he was squirming in his seat and grinning from ear to ear.

"What's wrong with *him*?" asked William, pointing.

"I think he may have fleas," said Melanie. "Fleas and my Nancy Drew books. That's the worst kind of guest, if you ask me."

"They're not *your* Nancy Drew books," said Turgid. "*He* won them!"

"Yes, but I clearly had dibs on them and I live here. Who is he, just some scarecrow of a boy you scooped off the lawn!" said Melanie, her eyes blazing.

"Would you like them back?" Rupert asked Melanie politely, getting off his chair and preparing to deliver them to her.

"Stop that right now!" barked Uncle Henry. "That's cheating! If Melanie wanted them, she shouldn't have lost them in Forfeit. You can't go around just *giving* things to people! Why, there'd be chaos! Anarchy! Bad things would come whiffling through the tulgey wood. I'm telling you, I won't have it at my game table!"

"Oh," said Rupert, and sat back down.

"Well, stand forewarned, I'm gunning for you," said Melanie, squinting at Rupert.

"Excellent! Now there's the attitude," said Uncle Henry.

Rupert looked sick.

"Never mind," said Turgid. "Soon you'll have a chance to win *all* the prizes."

More prizes, thought Rupert! *Had there ever* been *such a day?*

Mrs. Rivers insisted they have dessert before the final game, so everyone placed their prizes on the floor and Billingston reset the table and brought out all the pies and cakes and cookies and éclairs and custards again. Another hour was spent with concentrated stuffing. This time Rupert had room for it. He proceeded to make himself as ill on the sweets as he had on the savories. It was a wonderful kind of sickness. Finally, everything was cleared away for the last game of the day.

Uncle Henry sat down, looked around the table with narrowed eyes, and then brought a deck of cards out of his pocket with a flourish.

"It's poker," Turgid explained to Rupert. "And we play until there is one winner left who has won everything."

"You mean I can lose my prizes again?" asked Rupert. "The ones I won in all the other games?"

"Yep, you probably will too. Uncle Henry is a dynamite poker player. Same with Dad. Uncle Moffat's not bad. They've been playing for years. The rest of us are pretty much on an even playing field. Someone will end up walking away with everything at the end of the game. It's tough. But on the other hand, the prizes aren't the point, it's playing the game, right?"

No, thought Rupert, *it's the prizes.* He turned his head and looked at everything he'd won. He had a warm winter hat, a stuffed bear, two boxes of chocolates, a Monopoly game, a set of encyclopedias (he couldn't even *lift* all of those)—why, it would take a truck to get all of this home. He had dozens of things that he hadn't even gotten to examine properly yet. He almost wanted to ask if he couldn't just stop there for the day and keep what he had, but this, he felt, would be frowned upon. So he sat nervously at the table, his stomach making loud sounds from his gnawing anxiety and food overload.

Uncle Henry and Uncle Moffat tried to explain the rules in detail to Rupert while the others crowded around and shouted tips.

"We only play five-card draw," said Melanie.

"So it's not too complicated," said William.

"You don't play your hand; you play the people around you," said Mr. Rivers, which Rupert didn't understand at all.

"You must have a good poker face," said the other Turgid. "See, like this."

And he made such a terrible face that Rupert almost fell off his chair in fright and Turgid began laughing.

"All right, all right, enough, he gets it," said Uncle Henry. "Come on, deal the cards."

Rupert *didn't* get it though, not at first, and he lost

both the teddy bear and one of the most desired boxes of chocolates in the first two hands. Then desperation kicked in. When someone won a hand, they not only got their own wagered prize back, they got a pile of the other people's wagered prizes. His brain, usually unfed and so not good for much, was now on fire, tanked up with all the sugar and rested by its long time unused. It sprang into action for once and helped him out. He began to figure not just what to do with his cards but what was going on in everyone else's hand. He began to determine what the odds were that people's bets reflected the hand they actually had. He could not have told you how he was doing these things, but he was certainly doing them for he began to win. Every hand.

"He's cheating," complained William.

"That's enough, William," said Mrs. Rivers. "We never ever say that here."

"How could he cheat?" said Turgid. "He's never played before."

"That's what all cardsharps say," said William. "That's how they sucker you in."

"That's it," said Uncle Henry, standing up and glaring at William. "You're banned from the table."

"I don't care," said William. "I've lost all my prizes anyway," and he left to watch television and sulk.

"Don't mind him," said Uncle Henry. "He's always been a sore loser. But *you! You're* amazing! *You're* a genius. We've never seen anything like you. You've certainly livened up our Christmas this year. Yes, you have, young Rupert! What a special lad you are!"

Rupert blushed. Then he won again. He won until the area around his chair was simply stacked with prizes. He wondered again how he would get them all home. Perhaps the Riverses would let him make several trips. The most wonderful prize was the winter boots. He had been able to stand his freezing feet because he had no choice, but now, knowing that his feet would be warm, he couldn't bear the idea of them ever being cold again. It turned out you could bear things just until there was hope of reprieval. In horror, he realized that this actually made things worse, for now he had hope for something better. And hope was a terrible thing because it crushed the necessity of bearing the worst. And once the necessity was gone, so was the steely ability to do so. Now the thought of having freezing feet was unbearable and this was dangerous for he was not yet in the clear.

He and Uncle Henry were facing off for the last hand. Winner take all. Uncle Henry had a pile of enviable prizes on his side of the table as well. He'd won a saucer to go sledding. He'd won a skateboard. He'd won a case of canned corn. Rupert thought he would be happy to let Uncle Henry keep his prizes and all of his own too if only he could stop now and take the boots home. Just the boots. He would be happy just not to lose the boots.

Usually by this point the Riverses who were not in the final showdown had had about enough of each other and the games, and they drifted out to watch TV or read by the living room fire or have another go at the desserts. But this Christmas there was something about the electric energy between Uncle Henry, the expert, and Rupert, the novice—each determined to win, each spying the other with narrowed eyes over their cards—that kept everyone silently rooted to their chairs. Now all the prizes were heaped in one pile on the table, which fairly bent under the weight of them.

"Who will win? Who will win?" asked Mrs. Rivers nervously.

"Oh, do shut up, Beth," said Uncle Moffat.

"I want Rupert to win," said Turgid.

"Oh no, it must be Henry," said the librarian from behind the curtains. "It's always Henry."

"Oh, of course it must be Uncle Henry," said Melanie. "Then he can give me back my Nancy Drew books."

"Give up, you're not getting those books," sneered Rollin. "Even if Uncle Henry wins. Which he has to. Family honor is at stake."

"No, let the newcomer win," said Aunt Hazelnut. "This family could do with some shaking up."

Rupert and Uncle Henry said nothing. Their breathing

had slowed. Their eyes had narrowed even more. The room had shrunk to two card hands and a pile of prizes.

The winner won't be me, thought Rupert. *It can't be me. It* must *be me.*

Uncle Henry and Rupert each had five cards. They were allowed to throw out four cards from their hand to make a better hand, and to this end could ask for up to four new cards. Rupert had three sixes. Three of anything was good. Four was better. In fact, it would be unusual for anyone to get a hand better than four of a kind. But he had no idea what cards Uncle Henry held. If Uncle Henry asked for four new cards, he probably had nothing at all. If he asked for only one new card, it was likely his hand was very good.

Rupert asked for two more cards, discarding the two he had that were not sixes, hoping to get a fourth six. Uncle Moffat passed them to him. Rupert lifted the two cards one by one into his hand. The first one was a nine. But the second one, no, it was impossible. It was impossible! A fourth six! He would win! He would get to keep not just his own prizes but all of Uncle Henry's as well! But wait, not necessarily. *Let's not jump the gun,* he thought. It depended on Uncle Henry's hand and the cards he received. And now Uncle Henry was asking for two cards as well. Perhaps he had three of a kind. Perhaps he had three sevens and would get a fourth. That's all it would take for Uncle Henry to win. Four sevens.

Uncle Henry lifted the two cards he had received one by one into his hand as Rupert had, slowly revealing to himself what luck had brought him. Rupert studied Uncle Henry's face as intently as if it had the meaning of life written on it, but he could not tell what Uncle Henry had gotten. His face showed nothing.

Uncle Henry returned the stare. "Just two cards, eh?" he said finally. "You're bluffing, Rupert. I bet you have nothing in that hand. I bet it all."

"Yes, well, um, fine. I bet everything but the boots," said Rupert hopefully. After all, Uncle Henry might have any number of hands better than Rupert's. He might have a full house or a royal flush. Better in the end to err on the side of caution and keep back one prize.

"Don't be ridiculous!" said the other Turgid. "You can't do that. You have to meet his bet. You have to bet what he has and he has bet it all. So you must bet it all or forfeit it all. It comes to the same thing. Say it."

And then Rupert was surrounded.

"Say it! Say it! Say it! SAY IT! SAY IT! SAY IT!" they shouted until Rupert's head was swimming, his ears were ringing, and he could stand it no more.

"I BET IT ALL!" he exploded, because anything was better than this.

Then everyone was quiet.

"Players, reveal your hands," said Mr. Rivers.

Slowly Uncle Henry put his cards faceup on the table. Rupert looked at them. Then he looked again. At first, he was ill. Kings! Uncle Henry had kings. And kings were far higher than sixes. But wait. Could it be? Uncle Henry had, why he only had three!

Rupert put his own cards faceup on the table.

For a moment there was utter silence in the room and Rupert wondered sickly if they would pounce on him and kill him. That would be a not entirely unexpected ending to this day.

Then there was a huge shout and Uncle Henry shouted the loudest.

"FOUR SIXES! Brilliant! Brilliant! The boy is a genius! What LUCK he has! He's the luckiest boy I've ever known. Rupert, Rupert, you win, boy. You WIN IT ALL!"

Rupert sat as one who'd been hit with a hammer, but Uncle Henry paid no attention and continued to bounce in his chair.

"What a dark horse! What a surprise! I've never been so happy to lose in my life. What a game, eh, Moffat! What a game!"

Uncle Henry stood up and did a little jig. He and Uncle Moffat hooked elbows and danced about the room until they knocked over two wing chairs. They spun faster and faster until Uncle Henry was pulled right off the floor by Uncle Moffat's much heavier mass and he went spinning in a circle, his feet flying through the air, knocking bric-a-brac from tables and paintings off the walls. Finally, they fell over in a heap and lay on the ground laughing hysterically. Rupert was left sitting quietly alone. Wanting to laugh with them but barely able to breathe.

"You have won! You have won it all!" cried Uncle Henry, getting slowly back to his feet and trying to explain it to Rupert, whom he was sure hadn't understood, because he sat there so silent, so unmoving.

Everyone was cheering and punching Rupert jovially on the arm, trying to awaken him to his good fortune.

Then Melanie, who'd been sitting in a chair in the corner of the room, stood.

"Not quite," she said, looking more and more like a lizard to Rupert as she smiled a slow malicious smile.

"Oh dear," said Uncle Henry, sitting down and rubbing his head.

"Oh yes, oh dear," said Uncle Moffat, trying to sit up, but too fat and full at the moment to do so. He decided to remain lying for a few more minutes and gazed forlornly at the ceiling, repeating, "Oh dear, oh dear, oh dear. Yes, I'm afraid that's true."

Mr. Rivers looked away.

The cousins sighed.

Now they're all going to kill me, thought Rupert,

and perhaps *eat* me. He looked appealingly to Mrs. Rivers.

Mrs. Rivers wrung her hands nervously and then said, "Rupert dear, what Melanie means is that you have to answer one traditional Christmas question to really win. To really win and keep your prizes."

"*What?*" asked Rupert, and now he did come awake. *This* wasn't fair!

"It's just a little thing," said Mrs. Rivers.

"Hardly anything at all," said Melanie, her eyes sparking.

"Just a little tradition, as Mrs. Rivers said," said Mr. Rivers.

"*What?*" asked Rupert again, going pale.

"Oh, don't look so frightened," said William, who had returned to the room like a shark to the kill.

"We do it every year," said the other Turgid. "Billingston picks a question from the encyclopedia and the person who wins poker has to answer it correctly. If you do, you keep everything. If you don't, you lose everything."

"But . . . I already won," said Rupert, too disturbed by this turn of events to keep politely quiet.

"Not really," said Mr. Rivers.

"Not yet," said Melanie.

"Now, Melanie, he *has* won," said William. "But whether he will get to *keep* the winnings, that's the question."

"I'm sure he will," said Sippy.

"Not likely," said Rollin.

"I'm sure you'll answer the question correctly; you look like a bright enough fellow," said Mrs. Rivers, but she didn't look sure at all.

"Of course, you only get one chance," said William.

"One question," said Melanie.

"One answer," said the other Turgid.

"That will teach you to be a cheat," said William.

"Out!" said Uncle Henry. So William was once more banished from the fun.

"All right," said Rupert quietly. His brow broke out in a sweat. His hands shook. Mrs. Rivers fetched the envelope with this year's final question and held it nervously before her.

Everyone's eyes were on Rupert.

Mrs. Rivers looked at the circle of faces and took a deep breath.

"I hope," she said shakily as she opened the envelope, "that it will be an eensy bit easier than last year's question."

"That one was really impossible," said Uncle Henry. "It was idiotic. It was absurd. I lost everything. But anybody would have. It was a ridiculous question. I said to Billingston, you'd better stop coming up with such hard ones. Of course, he makes them hard because if the winner doesn't know the answer, we give Billingston all the prizes. So he has a stake in your failure, you see. But don't worry, boy." Uncle Henry leaned down and patted Rupert on the shoulder. "It won't happen to you. You're still in school. Your mind is fresh. Your brain cells aren't dead and blowing away like dandelion seeds. You'll have no trouble."

"Yes. Well!" Mrs. Rivers gathered herself and drew out the paper with the question. She read silently first. "Oh dear," she said, and frowned.

"What is it?" asked Uncle Moffat.

"It's—it's nothing," she said, and laughed nervously.

"Is it difficult?" asked Mr. Rivers.

"Not too difficult for our boy, Rupert, here," said Uncle Henry.

"Well, for God's sake, read it," said Aunt Hazelnut. "I can't stand here all day. I've eaten seven pieces of pie and I must lie down and digest."

"It's, um, geography this year," said Mrs. Rivers, clearing her throat. "Billingston has picked geography. He always picks such, um, difficult questions."

"Are you good at geography, boy?" asked Uncle Moffat.

"Of course, he is!" said Uncle Henry. "He's good at everything, our boy. Didn't you just see him skunk me at poker? A game he'd never played before?"

Rupert looked up hopefully. The thing was, he *was* good at geography. He was interested in the world because he planned to travel some day when he became a person who does a special thing, whatever that turned out to be. He had already memorized all the state capitals and had started on Canada. He knew the continents. This wasn't so bad. Thank goodness it wasn't a math question. He stopped trembling and pulled himself together.

"I'm ready," he said.

"Ahem, right, ahem," said Mrs. Rivers faintly. Despite everything, she still didn't look happy. She put the paper down and folded her hands. "Listen, perhaps Billingston could come up with another question, one a mite, and I say just a *mite*, easier."

"That's not the rules," said Melanie. "That's cheating."

"OUT!" said Uncle Henry, whipping around to glare at Melanie and pointing to the doorway.

"No, no," said Mrs. Rivers shakily. "She's right, she's, uh, up to a point, that is, well, it would be cheating. It's not fair to banish her for speaking the truth. Rupert, my dear . . . ?"

"Just *GET TO THE QUESTION!*" roared Uncle Moffat, who had hoisted himself to his feet, was getting sick of the whole business, and wanted his cigar.

"Right, right, then," said Mrs. Rivers, and giving Rupert a sympathetic smile, she read, "In what country can Huambo be found?"

"What?" asked Rupert in dismay. He didn't even

know what a huambo was. Was it a fruit? A building? A soft drink? A dance? No, this was geography, so it must be a place. Or did geography also cover things that were associated with places? Now it turned out he wasn't even sure what geography *covered*. This was a nightmare!

"That's an easy one," said Melanie, rolling her eyes.

"Everyone knows that," said the other Turgid, nastily gleaming. "You do, don't you, Rupert?"

"Can you read it again?" asked Rupert, quivering. If Melanie and the other Turgid thought it was an easy question, perhaps in his nervousness he had heard wrong.

"No, I'm so sorry, that's not allowed," said Mrs. Rivers. "The rules state that I cannot repeat the question and you must be given no time to think of an answer, but seeing as how you're a newcomer to this game, we will give you thirty seconds."

"That's cheating..." began Uncle Henry, and then, because he liked Rupert so much, finished, "Oh, all right. A special dispensation by the rules committee. Only this one time. William, you may come back for the countdown."

"THIRTY, TWENTY-NINE, TWENTY-EIGHT, TWENTY-SEVEN..."

The family now swarmed around Rupert. William, who had returned, had eyes gleaming like a wild dog's. They chanted down together in one loud voice.

If Rupert had any chance of retrieving this piece of arcane information from the dim reaches of his brain, it was now gone. All he could come up with was the next number that they were about to shout out.

As the family chanted they closed in upon him tighter and tighter. Now they all seemed to be wild dogs and Rupert was the rabbit in the middle. Any second they would be upon him. His eyes fell on the boots. The boots! Could he grab them and run? He felt hot breath. He looked up at large staring eyes. The room was suddenly too warm. He was too full of food. He thought he might vomit.

"TEN, NINE, EIGHT..."

Rupert looked at the ground. And then, like a small flicker of light he heard the word again. *Huambo*. And something, some light went on in his brain. It whispered to him, *familiar*. Familiar? Something... He had *seen* that word on a map somewhere. He could see the map. And on it a large continent. Which one? North America? No. Asia? No.

The room was swirling in waves, the bodies around him seemed to be bending like trees in the wind.

"SEVEN, SIX..."

And then he remembered. Africa! Once he'd been called to sit outside the principal's office because John and Dirk had stolen the school secretary's cat. He'd spent two hours on a hard bench as the principal tried to determine whether Rupert had had any part in the caper. He had had nothing to do and across from him on the cinder-block wall had been a map of Africa.

"FIVE, FOUR..."

Rupert looked up one last time at all their faces, some excited, some disappointed, some wishing just for things to be done with so they could do something quieter. He looked at his pile of prizes. His sweaters, his Cookie of the Month Club membership, Elise's Nancy Drew books. THE BOOTS! *Please,* he begged his memory. Where *in Africa? Please!*

His mind made one last desperate plunging attempt to come through for him. To come through for those warm boots and Elise's books. He could see the shape of a country forming. He could see the letters on the map spelling out Huambo right in the middle of the country. Huambo was a city in that country he could vaguely remember from the map. *But what country?* he thought desperately. He saw letters forming on the map. He could almost see the name of the country. He would keep the books and the boots, after all!

But his brain had just enough life left to think of the country's name or imagine the warm boots and Rupert had spent that energy thinking of boots. He had one last image of fur-lined warmth and then the swirling was too much.

"THREE, TWO..."

Rupert fainted.

What seemed like a second later, his eyes snapped open and he whispered as loudly as he could from the prone position where he'd slid off his chair to the floor, "ANGOLA!"

But when he looked up half the Riverses were gone.

"Too late," said Melanie, smirking.

The family, who had been packed about him like a wall of eyes, had already strolled away. People were milling about, getting more dessert, and heading to the parlor to read or to watch TV.

"You lose," said William, bending down so he could proclaim this directly into Rupert's ear.

"But I got the right answer," protested Rupert groggily.

"Isn't that a shame?" said Mrs. Rivers. "You were so close. You almost got it in in time."

"This is the best game day we've ever had, isn't it?" said Uncle Henry. "The thrill of victory! The agony of defeat! It was *TENSE*, wasn't it? That's what you want out of game day. *Tension!*"

"It was gripping!" agreed Uncle Moffat.

He and Uncle Henry departed for the parlor to finally smoke their cigars.

Rupert watched them leave as if he couldn't quite believe the outcome. The librarian, who had come out from behind the curtains for the big moment, leaned over to where he lay and explained kindly, "You are thinking you were so close we should just give it to you. But we'd already allowed you an extra thirty seconds, you see. We couldn't do more for you than that."

"*You're* not part of the we of whom you speak," said Melanie to the librarian. "We hardly know you."

"Melanie, don't be rude," said Mrs. Rivers.

But the librarian went chastenedly back behind the curtains.

"This fainting is really a bear, isn't it?" said Turgid. "I mean, a most vexing habit, I'd say. It's certainly caught you out this time, hasn't it?"

"It's not constructive behavior," said Mr. Rivers from where he was polishing off the rest of the éclairs. "You ought to stop."

He picked up a pile of newspapers and left to read them in the solarium.

"Oh well, better luck next time, old chap," called Uncle Henry from his cloud of smoke in the parlor. "What a day! What a great day!"

"Would you like a cup of tea, dear?" asked Mrs. Rivers. "And perhaps a bit more cake?"

"I think it's time I went home," said Rupert, who could bear no more.

"I'm terribly sorry about how this turned out," said Turgid. "Could I have my clothes back, please?"

THE PLAN

AFTER RUPERT changed into his own clothes he tried to make his polite good-byes, but no one seemed much interested in him anymore. Some even seemed to not quite remember who he was. Mrs. Rivers and Turgid walked him to the door.

"Here, eat a chocolate," she said. "I was a nurse and I know to give fainting people sugar. It has a reviving effect."

Rupert swallowed the chocolate but no longer cared. His appetite was gone and chocolate's wondrous properties seemed gone as well. Sweets could no longer make him happy. He didn't think he could ever be happy again.

"You weren't a real nurse," called Uncle Henry from the parlor. "Tell him. You were only a nurse for Halloween one year. It hardly counts."

"It counts," Mrs. Rivers called back.

"Bye-bye," said Aunt Hazelnut, who was passing through and shoved Rupert out the door.

Billingston appeared after that and pressed the button by the front door to open the gate and then close it behind Rupert as he began his long, cold slog home. He could certainly have used the boots, he thought miserably as his sneakers, which had dried during the afternoon, quickly became wet again and then freezing cold. It made his toes hurt before they became blessedly numb.

Rupert made his way through the very rich part of Steelville where the six other mansions were tastefully decorated for the holidays. He could only imagine the meals, the presents, the prizes behind those elaborate gates. He passed through the merely rich neighborhood with its understated decorations. Next, he went by the pleasant, well-tended yards of Steelville's managers and teachers and business owners. Their porches were bright with Christmas lights and their windows showed warm scenes of family togetherness, bounty, and holiday cheer. Then he passed the poor but proud, neatly shoveled walkways of the factory workers. Here he passed lit trees in windows and the occasional polar bear inflatable. Finally, he got to his own part of town, where the lowliest of the factory workers lived or those who didn't work at all tried to survive. The scruffy houses sat on derelict lots with mountains of salty, dirty snow because the city plows dumped their full truckloads there. Rupert could see little but the blue lights of televisions as he passed by and heard nothing but the merryless silence.

Oh, why didn't I remember that Huambo was in Angola before I fainted? he thought miserably. *I'm so ignorant, slow, and stupid. I'm so useless.* Not only had he no boots but he had no books. He had no way to distract Elise from her hunger or cold during the long nights. But...of course! He did! He did have something. The favor from the cracker! He might not have books, but he had a deck of cards. He would learn the card games he saw other children play during their lunch hour—old maid, go fish, gin rummy—and teach them to her! And for tonight, not knowing those games, why he'd make up his own! Perhaps he would become famous for making up card games. Inventing games children all over the world would want to play! Maybe this was the special thing he would do! After all, he had won poker playing against Uncle Henry, who was the reigning champ. Uncle Henry had called him a genius! Maybe that's why he had only the card deck at the end of the day. Because making up games was to be his calling! Perhaps this was all meant to go precisely as it had for this very reason! He, Rupert Brown, was meant to be a game maker!

Rupert reached his hand excitedly into his pants pocket and felt around, but there was nothing there.

Too late he remembered putting the deck of cards

in Turgid's fleece pants, meaning to transfer it to his own later. He had forgotten. He was an idiot. He carried home nothing from this day but a full stomach. And although he *himself* was full, he had nothing to share with his family. He had failed them all.

And so he slogged up his porch steps.

When he got inside, his whole family was sitting around the television. He went to stand by Elise, who was curled up in a corner of the room where she could hear but not see the television. She was there because all the good spots in the small room had been taken and she was one of the littlest, easily shoved to the back.

"Everything we got in the basket had an expired pull date," complained his mother, reading the side of the can of shrimp pâté she was eating.

Rupert's little brother Josh was grabbing for it but Mrs. Brown batted him away. "Stop that," she said. "You got the expired smoked cauliflower." Then she looked at Rupert as if trying to remember where she'd seen him before. "I guess you missed the basket delivery. Now it's all gone, so don't bother asking for anything. Where did you go?"

"I forgot it was Christmas," said Rupert. "I went to school."

"HA! What a lame brain!" laughed John, a cat under his arm.

"Whose cat is *that*?" asked Rupert fearfully.

"Uh, no one's," said John, turning his head to look out the window.

"Shh," said Dirk. "Mom hasn't noticed yet."

"Yes, I have," said their mother nonchalantly. "I just don't throw cats on Christmas."

"Quiet! I want to hear this truck commercial," said his father. "Someday I'm gonna get one."

"No, you're not," said Rupert's mother. "You don't even have a job."

"No, I guess not," said Rupert's father, and slumped lower in his chair.

"There's nothing left from the Christmas turkey basket," whispered Elise. "But I saved you this." She handed Rupert the wishbone with a scrap of meat still clinging to it.

"That's okay," said Rupert, thinking of everything he'd eaten that day and feeling more than ever like a worm. He should have asked for something to bring home to her. A roll. A piece of pie. But he knew he couldn't face such embarrassment even for her. You couldn't just *ask* people for things. "You have it. I ate something while I was out."

"Really?" asked Elise. "What?"

"Come on, wish," said Rupert, changing the subject and taking one side of the wishbone. "And after that you can finish eating it."

Elise grabbed the other side and they pulled. Elise got the long end and so the wish.

"I wish it weren't so cold," she said, holding up her piece of bone with its last scrap of meat. The cat, spying this, leapt out of John's arms, deftly snatched away the bone, and took it off to finish for himself.

"You must promise me in future," said Rupert as they watched the cat walk out of the room, the bone sticking out of his mouth, "if you get a chance to eat, you will eat all you can without worrying about me. Don't save me anything. We have to eat when we can or you see what happens: the cat gets it."

"The cat," repeated Elise.

"Or something. Things get taken. Things get gone. That's what I discovered today. You can't hold on to things or you'll be disappointed."

"Okay," said Elise quietly, but she looked puzzled. She sat back down to listen to the television.

"Merry Christmas," said Rupert, standing up to go to bed.

"Merry what?" asked his mother, her mouth open, displaying half-chewed expired shrimp pâté. "Merry *Christmas*?" Then she laughed so hard some pâté fell onto the floor. The cat got this too.

"John and Dirk, you take that cat back where you found it," ordered Rupert's mother. "NOW."

John stood up, silently picked up the cat, and he and Dirk headed out the front door.

Everyone but Rupert turned back to the television.

He went to bed.

Eventually the living room floor became too cold even for sitting and watching television, and everyone else retired as well.

Under the bed, the cold of the house crept slowly in through Rupert's hole-ridden sweatshirt, his three shirts, and his sparse flesh and entered his bones. He wrapped his one ragged blanket more tightly around him.

Rupert could hear the wind beginning to pick up and whistle through the power lines in the charging station at the end of the block. It did not sound cozy. It sounded ominous. As if the electric lines might become long, tendrilly arms that would reach right through his bedroom window and *get* him. With this thought he fell asleep.

The next day and the next night were cold and windy and the next day and night after that, colder and windier still. Rupert couldn't wait for school to start and vacation to be over. At least at school he had six hours of good, normal heat. But the vacation days seemed to drag on endlessly until one windy night Dirk elbowed him awake and said, "You're closest to the window, go check on it. It sounds like the wind is blowing rocks into it."

"Even if it is," said Rupert groggily, "what am I supposed to do? I can't stop the wind."

"I don't know," said Dirk. "But it's driving me crazy. Think of something or I'm going to kick you." Then he fell back asleep.

Rupert got up. Perhaps he could find some cardboard to tape against the window, although what they really needed was something on the *outside* of the window. He was still in a half-asleep state as he thought about this. Maybe that's why people had shutters. What kind of gale picked up rocks and flung them? Perhaps it was ice pellets, not rocks, hitting the window. Perhaps they were having an ice storm. But how would he stop *that*?

When he looked out the window he could see nothing at first except snow falling and being blown in eddies down the street. Then he saw something else. Lights from a car parked in front of the house and a dark figure standing below. A figure raising its arm and, yes, flinging rocks at his bedroom window. This made no sense at all. Rupert wanted to open the window to call out, but the window frame was so old and rotted it might never close again. If he wanted to ask this figure why it was throwing rocks, he would have to go outside.

Rupert crept downstairs, put his sneakers on, and went out the front door.

"Rupert, thank goodness," said the bundled-up figure.

"Mrs. Rivers!" said Rupert in surprise, and could think of nothing else to say. She was perhaps the last person he expected to find throwing rocks at his window.

"Yes, come along, dear," she said, indicating her car, its engine still running.

This whole sequence of events was odd, but at least it offered an opportunity to be warm, thought Rupert. He tripped sleepily over to the car and they got in.

"I was so worried I had the wrong window," said Mrs. Rivers. "But I've been watching your house for two days and there seemed to be only three bedrooms. The front ones and the back and I've seen a boy's face at the left-hand side front window so I figured that must be the one you slept in and your parents must be at the back."

Rupert nodded.

"Well, good. I always did think I would make an excellent detective," said Mrs. Rivers. "Now, let's get going."

She put the car in gear and pulled onto the street.

"Where are we going?" asked Rupert in alarm.

"We're going to have a little adventure," said Mrs. Rivers.

"What if someone wakes up and notices I'm gone?" asked Rupert, looking frantically out the back window, expecting to see people dashing out the door and gesticulating at the disappearing car. It was one thing to be gone all Christmas *day* and another thing to be driven off somewhere at night.

"If they didn't catch you going down the stairs and outside, it's doubtful anyone will notice," said Mrs. Rivers. "I speak from experience. I go out every Tuesday night and don't come back until dawn and so far no one has noticed me missing. I often wonder if my absence would be noticed if I lived in a smaller family. There's something about so many people living together that makes it easier to slip out. Be grateful for small blessings, Rupert."

They drove to the edge of town, and now she turned the car onto the road that took them to the highway ramp.

"Rupert dear, is that the same hole-ridden sweatshirt I saw you depart in at Christmas?"

"Yes," said Rupert.

"Well, that won't do. You can't go into Zefferelli's wearing *that*."

"Zefferelli's?"

"It's a restaurant in Cincinnati. A very smart restaurant. People dress up."

"Why are we going to a restaurant in Cincinnati?" asked Rupert, growing more and more concerned. Every time he saw this family, strange things seemed to be afoot. Strange to *him* at least. He was always worried that people thought his family peculiar for cat stealing, but perhaps in the larger world peculiarities abounded. Perhaps cat stealing was *nothing*.

"Mr. Rivers and I go there every year for our anniversary and it's where I now go every Tuesday night. It's a wonderful restaurant. Great food. So when I decided I wanted to be a chef, that's the restaurant that came to mind. I mentioned this to Mr. Rivers, who said he didn't like the idea of a wife who worked. He said it would make him look bad at the club. He said that there would be whispering that he could not support his wife. That our fortune was falling. Because if he could and it wasn't, why was his wife becoming a cook? Not a *cook*, I corrected him, someday a *chef*. Although, really, I wouldn't mind being a cook either. Have my own little diner. That might be fun too.

"Now I know in this day of women's rights you would think we were beyond that. You would think I wouldn't tolerate such an attitude, but marriages are complicated things, Rupert. With their own pacts and war zones and unspoken contracts, and I wasn't ready to go to war about this. So I decided I would just have to learn to cook behind Mr. Rivers's back. Then I came up with a plan. Cooking school was out. I could hardly do that secretly. I needed a restaurant that I could sneak into at night and learn the trade. And where else but Zefferelli's? I asked the head chef, Chef Michaels, at Zefferelli's, if I could hang out in the kitchen nights and he said, yes, but only on Tuesdays, because they're not quite so crazy as on the weekend with lines at the door. I've learned a lot, Rupert. At first, I just watched the cooks on the line and tried to stay out of their way. Then one night one of the cooks couldn't come in, so I convinced Chef Michaels to let me take the absent cook's place, and I did such a good job that now he lets me come in and take over someone's station or cook on the line in the later part of the evening so that one of the cooks can go home early."

"What's the line?" asked Rupert.

"That's a bunch of cooks all standing next to each other who make whatever the head chef tells them to. He might have a cook making a steak au poivre every time an order for it comes in. Steak au poivre after steak au poivre after steak au poivre. It's not inspiring work, Rupert. Not unless you're simply in *love* with cooking steak au poivre. Now, I realize that any kind of work, even artistic work like cooking or ballet, has its share of grind. Something you have to do over and over and over until it's in your BLOOD. I'm sure ballerinas are half the time flitting across the stage looking all ethereal but saying to themselves, 'Oh, pas de chat, pas de chat, pas de chat—when does it ever *end*?' That's how I began to feel about steak au poivre if you want the truth. And that's why I decided cooking on the line would never be enough for me. I want to *create* the dishes that Zefferelli's serves, not simply implement them. That's where my true talent lies. So I've hatched yet another plan. It turns out, Rupert, I'm very good at plans. This one kills two birds with one stone. But you never know these things if you don't spread your wings and fly, do you, Rupert, *do you*?"

Mrs. Rivers went back to driving with a little smile on her face. Rupert felt some response was required from him, but he really did not know what. Finally, he just said, "That's very nice, Mrs. Rivers."

"Why, thank you, Rupert," she replied.

They sped along down the highway for a while in silence. The sea of lights coming toward them through the snow was obscurely reassuring. Rupert liked Mrs. Rivers, but he wasn't sure he wanted to be alone on the road in the car of someone who had gotten him up so late and driven him smiling and thinking of other things to someplace she wasn't supposed to be. It all had a vaguely dangerous air about it. Not menacing but off the rails. Rupert always tried to be very very good. Off the rails was not his style.

As they drove, Rupert grew sleepy again. He was thawing out. In fact, he was growing warmer and warmer. Did he have a fever? His back was particularly warm. It felt lovely, his muscles melting into the seat. Could you be so feverish that you simply melted? Rupert remembered his teacher's first aid lesson about hypothermia—that people with hypothermia, as their body temperature dangerously dropped, often got very comfortable and felt warm. In fact, sometimes so warm that they ripped off all their clothes, thus hastening freezing to death. Was this what was happening to him? Suppose next he had the uncontrollable urge to rip off all his clothes? Here in the car with Mrs. Rivers! Should he warn Mrs. Rivers that this was impending? But what could he say? *Mrs. Rivers, I don't want to alarm you but any moment I might have the irresistible urge to strip to my socks?* No, no, there must be a better way.

Finally he blurted out, "Mrs. Rivers, I think I may have half a fever. My front is fine, I don't think I am yet in danger of hypothermia, but my back seems to be heating up. And it may spread."

He felt this covered the situation.

Mrs. Rivers didn't take her eyes off the road, just said mildly, "Yes, I have seat warmers. If you're too warm, there's a control on your side, right there on the dashboard."

She pointed.

Seat warmers! And here he'd been worried that among other things he might be about to burst into flames!

"Wow," he said. "This is great. I wish there were such a thing as floor warmers." How handy this would be at home for his cold nights under the bed. Mind you, if his family could afford floor warmers, they could probably afford enough beds and the rooms to keep them in. And more heat.

"They do have floor warmers. Mr. Rivers had them put in in the bathrooms," said Mrs. Rivers. "I'm not such a fan, myself. I like a good cold floor."

"Wow," Rupert said again.

"Oh, brave new world," said Mrs. Rivers, and she seemed to be both laughing at and delighting in him at the same time.

Rupert didn't care. He was nodding off in the deliciousness of warm, relaxed muscles. He shook himself and tried to think of some conversation to stay awake. He had the uneasy feeling that he should stay alert during such an odd situation.

"Do Turgid or Rollin or Sippy or the cousins ever come with you like this?" he asked.

"No," said Mrs. Rivers.

Mrs. Rivers was a very intense driver, and she drove very fast, her hands at ten and two o'clock, gripped tightly around the steering wheel. She leaned forward as if trying to gaze as far down the road as she could and squeezed the wheel as if this were what was making the car go.

"You may think my children have unusual names," she reflected.

"Not so unusual really," said Rupert politely.

"You must have realized how the names Turgid and Rollin go with Rivers. Sippy doesn't go with Rivers unless you're thinking of someone drinking a river out of a sippy cup, but that's stretching things. I just liked the name Sippy. I'm afraid Turgid and Rollin were spite names. I kept suggesting names to my husband like Bill or John but they weren't grand enough for him. He wanted names that were in keeping with the old money of his family name. The Rivers helped found Steelville, you know. For a while they planned to call it Riversville, but old Josiah Rivers, who started the steelworks, refused. He wanted the name Steelville because he thought it would attract more workers. He wanted word to spread through the Kentucky hills that there were jobs to be had in the steelworks of Ohio and he thought calling the town Steelville was the best advertisement for that. Of course, he was right."

"My parents' families are from Kentucky," said Rupert.

"Well, there you go," said Mrs. Rivers, nodding. "Many of the Rivers through the generations have been important. They have monuments built to them. In steel. There is a steel statue of Josiah Rivers in the center of town."

"I know," said Rupert.

His class took a field trip there every year. The school had two field trips they sent the children on annually. The first was to the statue of Josiah Rivers. "Because of him you may be lucky enough to work in his steelworks one day," the teachers always said.

The other was to the steelworks.

Those two field trips seemed to cover everything the children needed to know about their futures.

"It annoyed me, the importance he put on giving them old money names," Mrs. Rivers went on, "because I didn't want my children to be simply the representatives of old money. I wanted them to be whoever they wanted to be. So after Mr. Rivers had nixed Francis and Martin and Edward, I threw out the name Rollin. As a joke, you know. Rollin Rivers. But he didn't get it. He wasn't putting it together. He *liked* the name Rollin. He *insisted* on it in the end. And when the next boy came along I playfully suggested Turgid, thinking surely he would get the joke this time. But he didn't. He loved it. He thought Turgid sounded medi-eval. And knightly. And that's when I realized that I'd married an idiot. Someone with no sense of humor at all. And although he's very smart in a *business* kind of way, he hasn't the kind of intelligence that maybe I should have been looking for. So my advice to you, Rupert, when you finally start looking for a mate, is don't just think about how cute some girl looks in her blue jeans, consider the kind of *conversation* you're going to have to have with her for the next fifty years."

"Did you ever think of...divorce?" asked Rupert tentatively. This seemed like a rather impertinent ques-tion to ask a grown-up, but he wished to be helpful and many of his classmates had divorced parents.

"No, no, the name thing? Water under the bridge. You can't go around divorcing people just because you can't stand to talk to them. But by the time Sippy came along I'd tired of the joke. And I was beginning to think about the boys' futures and how their names might affect them. Have you ever noticed, Rupert, them being beaten up in the schoolyard because of those names?"

"I can't honestly say I have," said Rupert.

"Well, that's lucky. I regret terribly having been so silly about it all. You can't imagine how you look back down the decades, years, or months even to the you of the past and say to yourself, What a jerk! I have always wanted to be a good mother to my children and that was not a very good start. I hope I have made up for it since."

"I'm sure you have," said Rupert kindly. "Turgid certainly seems to like you."

"Children should like their mothers," said Mrs. Rivers musingly.

"Indeed," he said again just for something to say. He wasn't used to using the word indeed, but he found himself being a bit stilted in conversation with someone grown up and so rich. He worried his natural vernacular wasn't equal to the occasion.

So far, whatever they were doing, whatever venture Mrs. Rivers had taken him on, seemed a bit cracked, but he liked her. She was kind. Despite the way she talked about Mr. Rivers, she had a comforting, easy-going, plump goodness about her. Like a big old blond bear squinting to puzzle out the world constantly and trying to find a way to make it work for everyone.

"And to further elaborate on your question," Mrs. Rivers continued, "no, I have never taken any of the children or anyone in the family or anyone at all to the restaurant at night with me. Nobody knows about this but you."

And then amid the blowing snow and trucks hurtling by, Mrs. Rivers seemed to make a sudden spontaneous decision and with a jerk turned the wheel of the car and drove right off the highway.

Rupert grabbed the center console with both hands and hung on in terror as the car skidded on the icy pavement and finally came to a swerving stop on the shoulder.

"Really, dear," said Mrs. Rivers mildly, "you'd think you'd never been in a car before."

She put it in park but kept it running, then turned to Rupert and gave him a long look as she tried to think of how to phrase what she wanted to say.

"Rupert," she said finally, "perhaps it is time I explained to you what you are doing here. I felt terrible on Christmas when you, a guest in my house, met with the crushing defeat of losing all those nice prizes you'd spent the day accumulating. I know you felt you'd won them fair and square, and you *had* won them fair and square, so losing them must have come as a surprise. A horrid one. I felt for you, I truly did. I know Henry says that I mustn't. That I've no business feeling for you. That the only thing that makes the games exciting and fun is the prospect of terrible disappointment. There must be a chance that you will fail miserably or success means nothing. Kindness means nothing without the reality of cruelty. Et cetera. And to that end we are never allowed to break any of the rules of the games or make exceptions. Some people win. Some people lose. That's just the way it is. Some people get bitter, some get determined, some are elated, some are depressed. But the games remain the games. I understand all that. I even, for the most part, agree with it. And I know Henry did finally allow for the extra thirty seconds, but what, I ask you, are thirty seconds in the scheme of things? So I felt for you. After all, *you* were not familiar with our ways. We could hardly expect you to walk into our home and understand such a philosophy right off the bat. I believed, in a word, you'd been shafted. So I decided to secretly make amends. I said to myself, I'll take him to Zefferelli's. That will make things right. And that is why you are here. In part."

She nodded to herself, put the car back into gear, pulled onto the highway, and drove onward to Cincinnati.

Rupert fell asleep for a while after that. He could not help it; the ride was so long and the car so warm and he was not used to being awake at this hour. He awoke when he sensed the car slowing. They were no longer on the highway but going down a ramp into city traffic. It had stopped snowing and to Rupert, who had never been out of Steelville, Cincinnati looked like a fairyland. He had never seen so many lights in his life. Or such big buildings and so many of them! There were people out everywhere despite the late hour. Some of them looked very sketchy even by Steelville standards, lounging about on icy sidewalks. Others looked rich and prosperous and purposeful. But where were they all going at such an hour? What were they all doing?

Mrs. Rivers and Rupert drove up and down city streets. Rupert had his nosed pressed to the window. He could have driven like this forever. The world was so much bigger than he knew. Of course, he knew everywhere was not like Steelville, but until you were out into it, you couldn't imagine, you couldn't *imagine* how small your own world was, how little you knew. It made him feel very peculiar. It disoriented him. All of these people who looked so different, who had lives so different from his own, thought their worlds were real too. And their Rupertless worlds *were* real.

For some reason, this scared the pants off him. Suddenly he had seen enough. He wanted to go home and get back under his bed. Fortunately, at that moment Mrs. Rivers turned into an underground parking lot, and Rupert was saved from the crowds of too many different people with too many different true lives and pulled into the quiet dimness below.

"Here we are," Mrs. Rivers said briskly as she parked the car. "Come on."

She exited, walked around and opened his door, grabbed his arm, and ushered him out from where he had been sitting thinking, *Let's just stay here in the quiet dark.* Then she surveyed him again critically.

"I really can't take you into the restaurant looking like this. What are we going to do? We're in a pickle, Rupert." She frowned and her squinty eyes got even squintier. Then she brightened. "I know. I'll find you the smallest chef's coat I can and tailor it. People will think it's some kind of strange costume, no doubt, but I'm handy with scissors and pins and at least you won't sit there with holes in your clothes. But we must hurry because I'm late relieving one of the cooks. Chef Michaels has got a temper. All chefs have tempers, I am told. Maybe it's the hot stoves. Maybe it's the pressure of getting so many dinners out on time. Maybe it's that people who want to cook for a living are unhinged. Anyhow, I can't risk being fired. Not tonight. Not the night of *the plan*. Come on."

Mrs. Rivers practically pulled Rupert off his feet rushing him through the back door of the restaurant into the kitchen. She seemed to be a different person here at Zefferelli's. Back at her house in Steelville she was quiet and nervous and motherly. But here she was decided and full of energy. She gave merry waves and hugs and greetings to all the staff as she and Rupert raced along. It was bedlam: sizzling food on grills, pans of things bubbling over, the shouted voices of the cooks along the line. Waiters ran through the kitchen door and pinned up orders with screeches of "Why isn't table thirteen's chicken ready?" Cooks ran behind the line shouting "Behind, behind, behind," as they went to the walk-in cooler for ingredients. Mrs. Rivers seemed unfazed by it all.

"What took you so long? I was supposed to go home an hour ago," said a cook to Mrs. Rivers as they ran behind him. "I covered for you by telling Chef Michaels that I asked you to come in late tonight so I could stay on a bit, but shake a leg now! I want to get out of here!"

"You're the best," said Mrs. Rivers. "I'll just be a tick."

She hustled Rupert along until she got him into the changing room. There she quickly found a small chef's coat hanging on a hook and then flagged down a waitress.

"Harriet dear, do you have any pins with you? A scissors?"

"Jeez, Mrs. Rivers," said the waitress, "I'm being run off my feet as it is. I've got some pins in my makeup bag but I don't have time to get them for you."

"Just tell me where it is. And where I can find a scissors."

"Back third cubby," said the waitress. "And for scissors, grab some poultry shears. But not from Andrew's station. He's in a mood tonight. He's messed up three of my orders on purpose already."

"The jerk," said Mrs. Rivers. She fetched poultry sheers and got the pins from Harriet's makeup bag and put the chef's coat over Rupert's emaciated frame. It was quite long. More of a dress than a coat. She knelt down on the floor and did some cutting and pinning, then leaned back to survey her work. "It will have to do," she said.

"Now, as I have said, I have a plan." Mrs. Rivers put her hands on Rupert's shoulders and looked him in the eye. "You are here because I felt bad about the prizes. But also because I need you. Here is what I want you to do."

She whispered it all into Rupert's ear.

After that Mrs. Rivers took Rupert to the front of the restaurant. This was a symphony of different sounds. It was less stressed-sounding and more excited. It was the sound of many people happily talking loudly to each other in order to be heard over the general din. There were the gleeful shouts of celebration and release from the humdrum world. Dishes and forks and glasses made clanking sounds as they hit the table where waiters put them down, and there was the whoosh of air moving as waiters glided like whales through currents in the sea. The restaurant was dim except for the candles alight on all the tables and the flash of metal and mirror from the bar area. It all smelled exotically wonderful of butter and garlic and spices and fresh bread and hot meats. It made Rupert dizzy, the smells and sounds and speed. It was all he could do not to grab a basket of steaming rolls as a waiter put them on a nearby table. But Mrs. Rivers continued, yanking him along in her great hurry until they got to the bar.

There she indicated the end bar stool, and while he clambered up she said to the bartender, "Sam, I'm babysitting young Rupert here tonight. I can't take him into the kitchen. Can you imagine Chef Michaels?"

Sam rolled his eyes and nodded.

"Be a nice guy and let him stay here. He's very quiet and he'll be no trouble."

"Well, all right, but the bar's busy tonight," said Sam. "I can't be looking after him."

"No, no, he's ten. He doesn't need watching like a four-year-old. Just let him sit here."

"You'll sit there quiet, Rupert, and cause me no trouble?" asked Sam.

"Yes, sir," said Rupert.

Then a customer flagged Sam and he was off to the other end of the long bar.

"I've got to go." Mrs. Rivers looked around distractedly and then swung Rupert's bar stool so he faced her squarely, put both hands on either side of his face, and said clearly and precisely. "Now...DON'T... FORGET!"

"But..." protested Rupert, for he had no idea, *no* idea at all, how he would do what Mrs. Rivers had asked him. Oh, this was a disaster. He should never have come. He wasn't made for this type of thing. He was going to disappoint her terribly.

He sat on his stool and fidgeted. Because the stool swiveled he found he could turn this way and that to see the entire restaurant. He could also quietly spy on the people eating, his back to the restaurant, watching them in the mirror over the bar. After a half hour though, this palled. The stool had no back, so there was nothing to lean against. He was tired, his back hurt from sitting upright, and he wanted to go to bed. He was so tired he finally leaned forward and put his cheek on the bar. When Sam got a glimpse of this, he threw Rupert such a look from the other end of the bar that Rupert sat bolt upright again. This caused Sam to laugh, and when people stopped clamoring for drinks, Sam took a Coke and a bowl of peanuts down to Rupert saying, "Tough night, eh, kid? Pretty late for someone your age to be up. How're you going to concentrate in school tomorrow? But listen, you can't lie on the bar. Looks bad."

Then before Rupert could answer, a waitress ran over with a tray and signaled that she had a drink order for Sam to fill, and he was off again.

Rupert thought that Sam must not have children himself if he didn't know this was Christmas vacation and there was no school. He leaned his elbows on the bar and sipped his Coke. He finished the bowl of peanuts. It woke him up a bit and he began to survey the problem. Mrs. Rivers had been very clear when she explained her plan. But she had given him no clue as to how to execute it.

"This is how the restaurant works," she had said. "It has its menu on a big chalkboard. There each night posted in chalk are three appetizers, three main courses, and three desserts. Every night the dishes change, so everyone arriving for a meal must view the chalkboard before ordering. Now I, Rupert, have created a new appetizer. If I can somehow get it on the chalkboard without anyone noticing, and if people order my appetizer and it's successful, then Chef Michaels will have to see that I am more than a line cook. I am a talented, innovative chef. The problem is getting it onto the chalkboard without anyone noticing. I certainly can't go up to the chalkboard and start writing on it. I'd be out on my ear in seconds. So this is where *you* come in. You're so thin you're barely noticeable. This is why I have brought you. In addition to that whole thing with the prizes. If anyone can do this, Rupert, it is you. I am counting on you."

Rupert had been pleased even as he knew he was being flattered.

"You're my inside man," Mrs. Rivers had said, patting him on the shoulder fondly.

"I am not sure about this plan," he had tried to tell her.

"It's a caper, Rupert!" Mrs. Rivers had admonished him. "Man up! Let go! Let fly! Leave caution to the wind!"

"Suppose we are arrested?" he had asked.

"Unlikely," she had said, and that's when she led him into the restaurant proper and parked him on his bar stool. She didn't care to discuss the situation any further.

But now surveying the restaurant, Rupert thought she was wrong believing he wasn't conspicuous the way an adult would be. He was, if anything, even *more* conspicuous. He was very out of place. He looked like a small child in a lab coat.

He watched people come in, look at the menu, be seated, and then study it again as they ordered. The chalkboard, thought Rupert gloomily, was a focal point. There would be no time that it was not watched. He could not, as Mrs. Rivers had suggested, simply drag a chair over and quickly add TARRAGON SPARKLE SALAD to the list of appetizers. She had written this, her newly created dish, down for him so he would spell it correctly. Perhaps if it was only one word he had to write on the chalkboard he might have managed it, he thought. But TARRAGON SPARKLE SALAD was too long to be written in the blink of a patron's eye. No, if people were not to notice him, then something else was called for. A distraction. But how could you distract an entire roomful of people? Rupert could think of only one way. But it was such a crazy way.

In his head rang Mrs. River's stirring words: *Man up! Let go! Let fly! Leave caution to the wind!* Rupert had never done any of these things. He had always followed the rules. And where had it gotten him? His cold, starving life being afraid of the bullies at school and his mother at home.

And that is when Rupert stood up and screamed, "FIRE!"

FLOATING

AT FIRST nothing happened. There is always a pause in such circumstances while the unexpected alarm makes its way slowly to the brain. And then a woman just a few tables away from Rupert pushed her chair back and said in a voice so low it could hardly be heard, "Did someone yell fire?"

Rupert gripped the bar with both hands, waiting for someone to figure out it had been he and pick him up to throw him out the front door onto the icy sidewalk. As he looked frantically around the room his eye caught the window of the door into the kitchen and there was Mrs. Rivers's face, her eyes huge. But her face disappeared almost immediately again and the next thing that happened was that the kitchen door opened a crack and a hand appeared with a burning roll of toilet paper which it hurled under a nearby table. Smoke drifted up from under the table and suddenly the call of "FIRE!" was erupting around the room from the kinds of people who yell it in such circumstances. Shoving and racing for the door was happening from the kinds of people who do *that* in such circumstances. Delayed reactions and heroic heaving of the elderly out the door was happening by people who do *that* in such circumstances. But one way or the other, everyone was finding their way out the front door.

That was quick thinking, Mrs. Rivers, thought Rupert admiringly, for he realized she must have heard him and decided, No fire without smoke.

This was Rupert's chance! He dumped a glass of water onto the flaming toilet paper roll, grabbed it, and tossed it into the wastebasket behind the bar. Then he ran to the chalkboard, grabbed a chair to stand on, seized the chalk, and, while the restaurant was empty, climbed up and wrote as neatly as he could under the third appetizer: TARRAGON SPARKLE SALAD.

Next Rupert slipped outside, where he moved among the crowd whispering, "False alarm. Go back inside. False alarm." Soon this was being repeated by the grown-ups and they began to drift back into the restaurant in the embarrassed way people do after they have reacted perfectly sensibly to an emergency but then found out there *was* no emergency and are ashamed to have reacted at all.

It had happened so quickly that none of the cooks or Chef Michaels had been aware of the commotion. Only the wait staff who had been in the restaurant knew what had happened, and they had no time to care. They were too busy serving to be delayed by a little nonsense around a false alarm.

Everyone had lost interest in the fire. Everyone but the couple at table four, where the smoking toilet paper had been tossed.

"Who yelled fire, Gloria?" asked the man, whose name was Stanley.

"Well, it wasn't us, that's all I know, even though I did see smoke by my feet," said Gloria.

"Madam," said a waiter, bending over to look beneath the tablecloth, "there is nothing there now."

"Well, there *was*," she insisted again.

"Of course there was," said the waiter, mindful of his tip. "Very observant!"

"Well, I always have been observant, haven't I, Stanley?" asked Gloria.

"Why do there have to be fires everywhere we go?" asked Stanley grumpily.

"There's never been a fire anywhere we've been," said Gloria.

"Well, it seems like if it's not fire drills it's always something," said Stanley.

"You're just hungry," said Gloria.

"Of course, I am. I'm starving. I need to order."

They looked up to survey the chalkboard.

"What is that sparkly thing on the menu?" asked an old lady at the next table, reaching for her glasses.

"Oooh, Sparkle salad—I'll have that to start," said Gloria. "Why don't you have it too, Stanley? Chef Michaels has never had that on the menu. It must be something new."

"I don't know, I'm not much for sparkles," said Stanley. "It's not going to have sequins in it, is it? Or those horrible silver balls I keep telling you to stop putting on cupcakes."

"Oh, honestly, Stanley. Sequins. That's the whole trouble with men," said Gloria confidingly to the waiter. "They never want to try anything new."

"I couldn't agree more," said the waiter, despite the fact that he was also a man. "But might I say I also loathe sequins. Especially in my food."

"Right, well, just bring me the air-dried beef," said Stanley. "That's a manly starter."

And the restaurant fell back into its busy hum.

"Listen, kid," whispered Sam, slinking over to Rupert, "did you see who yelled fire? Did you see anything, because there's a roll of burnt toilet paper in the garbage back here! I think someone was trying to torch the joint!"

Rupert shook his head innocently and tried to look shocked.

Sam had been at the other end of the bar from

Rupert when he yelled fire but was one of the first to shove and push his way out the front door. "Women and children and the elderly first" meant nothing to him. He considered it an outdated concept.

"Whole thing's crazy," Sam began, but before he could continue, patrons began to belly up to the bar in a rush, as often happens after a scare. Sam was kept so busy after that that he had no time to dwell on who might have tried to set the restaurant on fire.

Mrs. Rivers had alerted all the cooks that in addition to the fried fish she was in charge of, she would be doing the sparkle salad station. No one else need make them.

When one of the waiters yelled "Sparkle salad" as he came in with an order, Chef Michaels said, "There's no sparkle salad on the menu. What—are you crazy? Go back and take the order again, you heard wrong."

But the restaurant was busy and he had no time to investigate further. This was what Mrs. Rivers had counted on and she happily began assembling her special salad.

Rupert watched the first two sparkle salads come out of the kitchen. They were bright green and on top there was a dusting of something pink and sparkly. The sparkle-dusted salads caught the candlelight from the tables, and because the restaurant was otherwise so dim, they glowed. *Why*, he thought, *they're beautiful.* He had never known food to look so magical.

The sparkle salads were placed in front of people at two tables on opposite sides of the restaurant.

"My, this looks yummy," said Gloria. She took a bite and groaned with pleasure. "Oh my God, Stanley. I've never tasted anything like this. You have to try it. It's fantastic!"

"Good lord, this is amazing, there isn't a word for what it is...it's..." began the woman across the room who was digging into her sparkle salad.

"Honestly, Lacey," said her husband. "You always tell *me* not to talk so much about my food."

"Well, to heck with that. *Taste* this," she said, and passed him a lettuce leaf.

His expression of irritation was replaced with ecstasy. "Give that to me," he said rudely, grabbing the plate and taking another heaping forkful.

Over at her table Gloria was still urging sparkle salad on Stanley.

At first Stanley objected, then through a full mouth he called out, "Waiter! More sparkle salad! Who wants a main dish when we could be eating *this*?"

At that, sparkle salad orders flew into the kitchen and sparkle salads flew out.

Rupert looked on in awe as the people who had ordered them began turning to people at other tables. To people they didn't even know, complete *strangers*, and saying, "You *must* order this. If you don't you will regret it. You will regret it for the rest of your lives!"

"Really," said a man. "I make it a point never to eat the food of complete strangers."

"Oh, shut up and try it," said a woman at the next table, leaning across the divide and shoving a forkful of sparkling lettuce into his mouth.

"Lady, lady, germs!" he screeched, but a second later he was saying, "MY GOD! Give me that. You can always order another. I want that one. I want that one *RIGHT NOW!*"

He got up and began to wrestle her for it. They each had two hands on the salad plate and were in danger of spilling the salad all over the floor when suddenly they froze in amazement.

Something even more astonishing was happening. Stanley and Gloria's table and chairs were beginning to rise. Slowly but surely they were heading for the ceiling with of course the people *in* those chairs rising as well.

"I feel most peculiar," said Gloria. "It's as if I'm made of air. As if I'm *lighter* than air."

"What is happening?" asked an old lady in another part of the restaurant as her table began to rise as well. "Margery, what is happening? In eighty-four years I've never risen in a restaurant this way. Is this the new trend? Do people float about now? I'm not sure I like it. I'm almost sure it should require seat belts."

"LIKE it?" said Stanley, whose table was hovering slightly below the ceiling. "I *LOVE* it. It's amazing. I've never felt so wonderful in my life. I'm a bird. I'm a plane. I'm SUPER STANLEY!"

More and more people had begun rising. One woman on the way to the restroom was rising even as she headed there. "Oh, my goodness," she said as she dangled by a light fixture.

Another woman who had been walking to the bar joined her. "Isn't this lovely?" she said. She found by gently flapping her arms she could swim through the air. "Isn't this divine?"

"No," said the woman who had been headed to the bathroom. "I have to pee."

All around the restaurant wherever sparkle salads had been consumed people were floating in midair.

"Is this really happening?" asked another woman. "Perhaps I am dreaming."

"No, don't you see?" said a woman in a feather boa. "It's the deliciousness of it. It's so fabulous, so delectable, so extraordinary that it makes you float. It makes you happy. You leave behind all your earthly concerns in the glory of it."

"That's *my* name," said Stanley's wife. "Gloria. Perhaps it all has something to do with *me*."

"Don't be ridiculous," said Stanley. "I've known you for thirty years and this is the first time I've ever known you to float."

Sam, who had stopped serving people, and Rupert, just stared in awe.

Where is Mrs. Rivers? thought Rupert. *She should see this.* He knew he was supposed to stay glued to his bar stool, but he couldn't stand the idea that she was missing the effect of her salads. So he jumped down, pushed through the door into the kitchen, and, grabbing her by her chef jacket, pulled her into the restaurant.

"Really, Rupert, what in the world..." she began, but her voice trailed off when she saw tables hovering beneath the ceiling.

Whatever she had expected, whatever results were to come from all the nights she had lain awake trying to invent a salad that would astound, she had not imagined this. She said nothing but clamped a hand down on Rupert's shoulder in sheer wonder, and the two of them stood like that, unable to speak a word.

Out of the blue a sadness overcame Rupert, as for a moment he wished it was his mother, not Mrs. Rivers, with her hand on his shoulder. He wished she were here with him to see this great thing. She worked so hard and always looked so tired. If she could see this, he felt sure it would spark something joyful in her. And for a moment he felt guilty that it was happening to him and not to her.

Then something dreadful happened. Chef Michaels, wondering why no one had ordered any of the steaks or fish or chicken on the menu and why all the line cooks who were supposed to prepare them stood idle, charged into the restaurant, looked up, and barked, "What's going on here? Just *WHAT'S* going on?"

"It's the sparkle salad!" said Gloria, giggling. "It makes you floaty. Try some."

"*What* sparkle salad?" asked Chef Michaels. "There was no sparkle salad on my menu."

"Well, there is now. Right here," said a woman floating high enough to put her finger on the chalkboard where Rupert had printed it.

Chef Michaels turned his attention to the chalkboard.

"That's not one of my salads!" he roared. "Who put that on my menu?"

"Whoever it was is a genius!" said a man from the ceiling. "You ought to listen to him. You ought to make him a head chef at the *least*."

"Balderdash!" bellowed Chef Michaels. "I ought to fire him! There is only one head chef and that is me! I will not *HAVE* this! Waiters, serve no more sparkle salads. And all of you! Get down right now. This is *MY* restaurant and I'll have no *FLOATING*! Who made these concoctions, anyhow? I'll have his head!"

"I did," said Mrs. Rivers in a small voice. "People seem to like them."

"We love them, dear," said the old lady who was now experimenting with doing loop de loops with her chair in the air. "I've never had such a feeling from a salad. Do you think it's the folic acid? I read that everyone should eat more folic acid. I certainly would have if I'd known this is what would happen."

"Mrs. Rivers, how dare you! Get out of my restaurant! And you people up there floating, that's against the rules. Get down. Get down RIGHT THIS MINUTE before I CALL THE POLICE!"

And just like that, all the tables, all the chairs, all the people drifted back down like balloons that had been pricked. No one was ready for this. They had just started to feel so . . . luscious.

There was a little sigh from the old lady, and then she said, "Initially I wasn't sure I liked it, but now that I'm down I want to go up again."

A terrible quiet came over Zefferelli's as everyone sat silent and deflated—all you could hear was the discontented scraping of chairs.

Gloria was the first to speak. "I guess the fun's over."

"I don't like this chef," said another patron.

"No, indeed," said another. "Who is he to spoil our fun?"

"Stanley, pay the bill and let's go," said Gloria, standing up and putting on her coat. "If I can't float, I don't even want to be here."

"Yes, the food was never that good anyway," said another man.

"Not before the sparkle salad," said a woman.

People were getting their bills, paying them, putting on their wraps, and heading for the door.

Chef Michaels looked about in continued fury and then headed into the kitchen, where Mrs. Rivers and Rupert, who had taken off his chef's coat, were quietly cleaning up the sparkle salad and the sauté stations.

"YOU!" he roared. "You fiend! You cursed woman! Making things that aren't on my menu is TREASON! It's...it's..." He paused, unable to think of a word for such a horrendous act. He looked at Mrs. Rivers as if determining what she would least like to be accused of and finally finished with, "It's BAD BEHAVIOR!"

"But people liked them!" Mrs. Rivers protested. She still hoped that once Chef Michaels thought it through, he would see how good this had been for business and promote her to chef.

Instead he yelled, "YOU!" again.

He was really not much of a word person.

Then, because he could think of nothing else to say, he grabbed a cleaver and began to wave it around threateningly. "YOU! I'LL SHOW YOU!"

"Oh! Oh!" cried Mrs. Rivers. "Please don't cut off my appendages! I've always found them so handy! Rupert, I don't wish to alarm you—whatever I expected in the way of a reaction, it was not this—but after giving it some thought, I think we had better RUN FOR OUR LIVES!"

She and Rupert dashed to the coat room with Chef Michaels hot on their trail. Mrs. Rivers grabbed her coat and purse, and they made for the door. Fortunately, Chef Michaels slipped on a puddle of grease and it gave Mrs. Rivers and Rupert just enough time to fly out the back kitchen door to the street.

Down the block they ran, with Chef Michaels in greasy shoes running and slipping on the icy side-walk behind them. Rupert was afraid to look at Mrs. Rivers. He was sure she would begin sobbing in dis-appointment any second, so it surprised him when he suddenly heard the gurgle of a laugh, and then she was running, slipping, and laughing, with uncontrolled mirth. Rupert had never heard anyone laugh quite like this. It was as if it had been stored inside her for years and had just now been released. Chef Michaels gave up chasing them a mere half block from the restaurant, but Mrs. Rivers and Rupert continued running until they'd circled the block and made their way to Mrs. Rivers's car in the underground parking lot. Once inside, Mrs. Rivers started her car with shaking hands, and drove like fury up the ramp and down the city streets, finally merging onto the highway to Steelville.

It wasn't until they were a good ways down the

highway that Rupert dared to look at Mrs. Rivers again. He was sure that no matter the laughter, the upshot of the evening events, where she had realized everything and then lost it again, would hit her any second. She would feel as he had when he had lost his prizes. But when he finally glanced at her, he was amazed to see instead that she looked elated.

"I loved how you yelled fire like that, Rupert!" she said. "That was perfect."

"And how you rolled the flaming toilet paper under that table!" said Rupert, joining in the happy post mortem in relief. "That was quick thinking!"

"Oh, Rupert! What an evening! The floating tables. The floating people! And the salads! They really sparkled just as I planned. You wouldn't think Himalayan sea salt and pink dusting sugar would perform such tricks!"

"No one will ever forget it," said Rupert. "*I* never will. Even if Chef Michaels thinks we behaved badly."

"He was right," said Mrs. Rivers. "We didn't behave well. We broke the rules. But I don't know, now I'm wondering, well, I don't really know how to express it, Rupert."

They drove silently for a bit and then she said, "Maybe bad behavior is only what we think other people are going to think. Maybe there is no absolute. Maybe we worry that we are doing things wrong when they're not wrong at all. I feel like the whole universe is much looser, more spacious and open-ended than we knew. Oh, Rupert, I like everything so much better now!"

Rupert was having his own thoughts, remembering everything that had happened that evening.

"I was selfish, going ahead and doing what I wanted," said Mrs. Rivers, shouting with laughter again. "And the world didn't end. Instead I'm *happy*! They don't tell you it will be like this! You think it will be quite the opposite, but it isn't!"

And she began to laugh again.

Happiness. It came like magic, out of the blue, like a burst of energy. Who knew where it came from? It was as if Mrs. Rivers had rung like a bell in the great echoing space of the universe. And she loved not just her own sound but the space she rang in. She loved it all.

And looking at her, Rupert had one more moment when he was sad that it was Mrs. Rivers and not his mother who had been freed by the wildness of the night.

For she rolled down her window so the cold air blew through the car. It blew what short hair she had behind her. The sky was crystal clear. Her face was alight. She sparkled from every inch. As if she'd eaten the stars.

THE TIME MACHINE

BUT THEN of course the cold returned. Heated seats were a thing of the past. Christmas was done and January hammered them. Snowstorms came one after the other and Rupert's feet never seemed to thaw. In order to bear it, he thumbed through his memories of the restaurant. He found this kept him going for the first couple of weeks, but as temperatures dropped lower Rupert's memories of the restaurant began to fade. The walk home from school was particularly exhausting.

He was plodding past the Riverses' house one day when he heard, "YOU, BOY!"

Rupert stopped to look, but all he could see was the thick, snow-covered, impenetrable, perfectly manicured hedge.

"I said, YOU BOY!"

Surely the voice didn't mean *him*?

He started to trudge again when the voice said,

"What's the matter with you? Are you deaf? Stop plodding and poke an arm through the hedge."

Rupert was startled, but he did as he was told and a hand grabbed him and pulled him the rest of the way through.

"HA!" said Uncle Henry. "Caught you!"

"How did you know it was me going by?" asked Rupert.

"I've been spying on you," said Uncle Henry. "I invented a hedge periscope and I said to myself, I bet Rupert would appreciate this. I showed it first to Turgid and Rollin and Sippy, but they had no interest. I didn't even bother with their cousins, ole whatstheirnames."

"Melanie, William, and the other Turgid?" said Rupert.

"Right. That's when I thought of you. I thought, if there's one thing Rupert would appreciate, it's a good hedge periscope. Too bad he doesn't live here. Then I used it to lie in wait for you. Come on, have a look."

Rupert approached the long-necked instrument that sat on a tripod. Looking through the lens he could see up and over the top of the hedge to everything that happened on the sidewalk below.

"Isn't this a great invention?" asked Uncle Henry. "And I thought of it myself."

"Yes, it's wonderful. Thank you for showing it to

me," said Rupert politely. He really needed to keep moving if he wasn't going to turn into a human popsicle. "Well, I'd better go on home."

"You're shivering!" said Uncle Henry, suddenly noticing. "Why aren't you wearing more clothes? A coat! A coat is conventional wear in January, Rupert."

"I haven't got one," said Rupert before he thought. Then he blushed bright red.

"That's unusual," said Uncle Henry.

"I'd better go," said Rupert again.

"You can't go," said Uncle Henry. "Not yet. You haven't seen my really special invention. It was to catch you that I specifically invented the hedge periscope. It was to catch you and take you up to the attic to see my really, *really* special invention. The one of which I'm most proud. And why, you ask? Why did I choose you to show it to when I haven't shown it to anyone else yet? Why *you*? Go ahead and ask."

"Okay, why me?" asked Rupert as Uncle Henry marched him through the front door and up the seven flights of stairs to the attic.

"Because, my boy, I felt bad, very bad about Christmas. Can you guess why?"

"The prizes?" asked Rupert.

"No. That's just the rules. You can't go around feeling bad about what happens after you've set up the rules. No, it was because I realized you'd left before we had the Christmas pudding. We totally forgot to keep you around for that. And I think you would have liked it. All plummy, lit up with brandy. On fire! I said to myself, a dessert that's on *FIRE* is exactly the kind of thing Rupert would love. Oh, I've got your number, boy. But selfish oafs that we are, we forgot to keep you around for it, and now it's gone and we won't have another one for a year at least. I must make it up to Rupert, I said to myself. I will show him *THIS*!"

They had reached the middle of the attic and Uncle Henry waved a hand theatrically down and forward as if presenting something. Rupert, for the life of him, could not see what Uncle Henry was pointing to. All that was before him was a large cardboard box.

"Is the invention in the box?" Rupert asked. He was stamping his feet as the circulation returned to his toes. They hurt terribly when this happened and he found he got over it faster if he stamped around.

"Stop that clunking about. No, the invention isn't *in* the box. The invention *is* the box."

"Oh. Well, it's a very nice box." Rupert floundered around for the appropriate response. "Good inventing. Do you plan to ship something in it?"

"Are you *CRAZY*? I haven't invented a *box*. The box has already been invented, otherwise how would you know what it was? You're losing it, Rupert. What small wit and intelligence you possess is drying up like a puddle in the sun."

"You said at Christmas I was a genius," protested Rupert before he could stop himself, because he had savored that remark ever since Uncle Henry had made it and it had warmed him on the nights when he was too cold to sleep.

"That was Christmas," said Uncle Henry crisply. "One is rather given to hyperbole at Christmas. Possibly sherry is involved." Then Uncle Henry noticed Rupert's crestfallen face and said, "Well, perhaps you are just having a momentary lapse in genius. Maybe your brain cells have been freeze-dried due to your unfortunate aversion to outerwear."

"Well, what is it then?" asked Rupert finally, because however much he wished to prove his genius status again, he couldn't for the life of him imagine what this thing did.

"Well, I'd say that was obvious," said Uncle Henry. "It's a time machine."

"Oh," said Rupert. "How nice." But what he was thinking was that Uncle Henry was completely cracked. And how long did he have to stay politely looking at this box before he could get out of here?

"Ha. You don't believe me, do you? It's written all over your face. And *why*, may I ask, don't you believe me?"

"Because," said Rupert, deciding to come clean, "there's no such thing."

But then he remembered Zefferelli's floating tables. Had *that* really happened?

"I see. I see. Then I guess we'll just have to take a little time trip and show you," said Uncle Henry, prancing about and rubbing his hands together. "That's what we do with skeptics around *here*! Well, actually, we haven't done that before because I've never used the time machine before. This will be its maiden voyage."

"If you've never used it before, how do you know it works?" asked Rupert.

"How do I *KNOW*? How do I *KNOW*? Because I *invented* it. That's how. What a ridiculous question. Why would I invent something that didn't work? Now, where shall we go? Well, it doesn't matter where we want to go or to what time we want to visit because I couldn't figure out how to invent the gauge or whatever you'd need to point yourself to a certain time. But you have to admit that it's enough to have invented a time machine. You can hardly fault me for not inventing one with a gauge. *You* couldn't have done better. Now, come on, hop in, there's room for both of us. Hurry up. I haven't got all day. Or maybe I do! Ha! Maybe I have all the time in the world."

Rupert inwardly rolled his eyes. He would get into this carton with Uncle Henry and watch him be disappointed that nothing happened and then he would go home. He didn't want to be late for dinner. His father had a regular route for collecting kitchen scraps and he went to the Carlsbergs' on Thursdays. Everyone liked the Carlsbergs' refuse. It tended toward pizza crusts.

"Hurry up, hurry up," said Uncle Henry, who had already jumped into the carton. "I can feel it beginning. I can feel it warming up. You don't want to be left behind. Now where shall we go? Perhaps if we just say it out loud, the time machine will take us there. Yes, I have a feeling, an *intuition*, Rupert, that this is how it works. All great inventors intuit things. We are very special people. We fly by the seat of our pants. Now the tough question is, where would we like to go?"

"Cavemen times?" asked Rupert. When he was little he and his brothers used to watch re-runs of *The Flintstones*. He had always secretly wanted one of those foot-activated cars.

"No, we certainly don't want to go there," said Uncle Henry. "Dinosaurs." He touched the side of his nose to indicate keenness of mental perception. They thought again. "I know, Giverny. Let's go watch Monet paint water lilies."

Rupert thought if they were going through time they might do something a little more interesting than visit a bunch of flowers, but he didn't really believe they'd be going anywhere anyway.

"Agreed?" shouted Uncle Henry, waving one hand like a great magician about to perform his prize trick.

"Sure," said Rupert patiently.

Uncle Henry raised his arms over his head and with great pomp and a deep voice said, "Time Machine, take us to Giverny, France, to watch Monet paint water lilies!"

There was a whirring sound.

"QUICK!" yelled Uncle Henry. "It's about to leave! Jump in!"

Rupert didn't have Uncle Henry's long legs, so he needed help scrambling over the side of the box, and when Uncle Henry leaned over to pull Rupert in, he only got him halfway when the carton tipped over onto its side. Rupert was head down in the box, his face under one of Uncle Henry's feet and one of his wet tennis shoes poking Uncle Henry in the back. It was all very uncomfortable. Meanwhile, the box continued making whirring and whizzing sounds. When they stopped, Uncle Henry and Rupert were in such a tangle that for a moment Rupert didn't know whose feet were whose.

"Feel how warm it is?" asked Uncle Henry, his chin pressing into his chest, his shirt flapping over his mouth so that his words came out muffled. "It must be summertime in France. Oh, *pain au chocolat*! Oh, Champs-Élysées! *Parlez-vous*, Rupert, *parlez-vous*."

Uncle Henry slowly untangled himself from Rupert and crawled out of the box.

"Wait a second," said Uncle Henry. "This isn't France. This isn't a hundred years ago. This looks like the 1970s. Look at the bell-bottoms, look at the swimsuits. Look at all that ghastly paisley. Look at these people. Where the heck did this thing take us? Aw well, some kinks still in the machine, but at least it took us somewhere warm. A day at the beach, Rupert. Perhaps that's just what we need! The box *knows*." Uncle Henry put his finger aside his nose again in his favored gesture of acute mental perception.

Rupert crawled out swiftly and looked around. He was standing looking at a beach along what appeared to be a small lake.

"Where are we?" he asked.

And then he saw a big sign: CONEY ISLAND.

CONEY ISLAND

THERE WERE people running around in swim-suits. There were Ferris wheels and a roller coaster and a merry-go-round. Everywhere Rupert looked people were having wonderful sandy fun, watery fun, carnival fun. But Uncle Henry wasn't fixated on any of this. He started pulling Rupert along by his sleeve.

"Come on, come on," he entreated urgently.

"Where are we going?" demanded Rupert, who was being dragged almost off his feet when he only wanted to get his bearings for a few minutes.

"To find the boardwalk. Coney Island is the eating capital of North America, of pretty much the *world*, boy. I haven't been here since my youth. Where shall we start? Hot dog? Caramel apple? Cotton candy?"

"But where are we? Where *is* Coney Island?" asked Rupert.

"New York. That waterway down there past the trees? That's the Atlantic Ocean!"

"I'm seeing the Atlantic Ocean in the distance?" asked Rupert, his jaw dropping, for he could just make out a long line of water past the midway and a line of trees. He stopped to stare but Uncle Henry yanked him forward again. Somehow, thought Rupert, he had always imagined the ocean to be much larger. With waves and seagulls and lighthouses. This looked more like a big green park.

"Mr. Rivers," said Rupert, panting as they ran along. He wanted hot dogs too, but something had just occurred to him.

"Call me Uncle Henry."

"Uncle Henry, should we just leave the time machine like that on the walkway? What if it gets wet?"

At that moment a muscular young man came bounding up and said to them, "My girlfriend wants to know if you came here in that box?" He pointed to the time machine where a young woman was bent over peering into it as if hoping to see a dashboard.

"In a *box*?" squealed Uncle Henry. "Are you mad?"

"Yeah, well, we were coming in the gate when you appeared suddenly in front of us. One minute you weren't there and the next you were," said the young man, looking embarrassed but truculent. He scuffed his tennis shoe on the walkway.

"Young man, you have clearly had too much sun," said Uncle Henry. "But you are correct in pointing out that piece of litter to us. Never litter, Rupert, keep

America clean. Fear not, young muscley man, my little friend and I shall remove the offending item. Rupert, chip-chop!"

Rupert and Uncle Henry ran back, and Uncle Henry rudely grabbed one end of the time machine to wrest it out of the girl's clutches as she turned it this way and that trying to devise its secret.

"Gimme that," said Uncle Henry. "Don't you know better than to pick up strange detritus? It might have bedbugs!"

The girl hung on to it. "Finders keepers," she said. "I saw this box with the two of you in it suddenly appear and I want to know the trick."

"If a box had suddenly appeared, do you think you'd be the only one interested? Hmmm? Don't you think it might have drawn a crowd? This is Coney Island, after all."

"My boyfriend saw it too," said the girl, stubbornly holding on to her end.

"My dear girl, your muscley young man is clearly suffering from the ill effects of overexercise. I'm a doctor and I should know. I would take him home right now if I were you and feed him a quantity of Jell-O. Good Jell-O, the kind you make yourself. Not that already made stuff."

"Are you really a doctor?" asked the girl, still gripping the box.

"Would I say I was if I wasn't?" asked Uncle Henry.

The girl said nothing, so Uncle Henry was forced to haul out the big guns.

"SPIDER!" he yelled. "Inside the box!!!"

The girl dropped her end immediately.

"Run, Rupert!" said Uncle Henry, and off they sped toward the water carrying the box. They ran until they were out of breath, hot and sweaty, and only then did they turn to see that the girl was leading her boyfriend to the parking lot.

Upon seeing this, Uncle Henry turned around and led Rupert back to the entrance of the park to get the lay of the land. There was a large midway to the left of the walkway. To the right was what appeared to be a small swimming lake with people splashing about. At the very end of the lengthy walkway beyond the trees they could make out a beach and a long strip of water. Sprinkled throughout were food stands.

"This is not the way I remember Coney Island, but then I was a young man when I was last here. By the time you are my age you will have forgotten all this too," said Uncle Henry cheerily.

"Oh, I doubt it," said Rupert, looking around in wonder.

"Anyhow, I am happy to see that that couple heeded my sound advice. A good bowl of Jell-O now and then will do more for them than all the push-ups in the world. Jell-O is fun. Now, Rupert, where to put this thing where it will be safe and waiting for us later? We don't want to spend the day carting it around. We want to go on rides after we eat."

"Oh," said Rupert in delight. "Do we really get to go on some of those rides, Uncle Henry?"

"Well, of course, what else do you propose we do here? Ah, just what we need!"

Uncle Henry charged over to the first hot dog stand they saw, where a man was carrying a pile of flattened out empty cartons that read BIEDERMEYERS HOT DOGS. He placed them behind a shed.

"Excellent," said Uncle Henry when the man had left. "We'll fold the time machine up and put it under this pile of hot dog cartons. We'll know it immediately, as it will be the only carton that doesn't say Biedermeyers Hot Dogs. Perfect. I'm a genius."

Rupert began to wonder if Uncle Henry called everyone a genius. "What if the garbagemen come and take away all the cartons?"

"I'm sure they don't come during the day," said Uncle Henry. "You'd never get a big garbage truck through this throng of people. They must collect it at night after the park closes. The time machine will be perfectly safe here."

Uncle Henry folded the time machine so that it was flat, lifted up the pile of collapsed Biedermeyer cartons, and slipped it underneath.

"Now!" He clapped his hands and rubbed them together. "What to eat? I suggest we be methodical about this. Let's go up and down the boardwalk and decide what we absolutely have to eat, what we want to eat, and what we will eat if we still have time. Then, with those choices in order, we eat three things, go for a ride, eat three things, go for a ride...Come, Rupert, don't dilly and don't dally. Let's find the boardwalk."

But although Rupert and Uncle Henry walked from one end of the park to the other, the boardwalk remained elusive.

"That's odd," said Uncle Henry. "When I was a lad and went to Coney Island, the boardwalk was the *thing*. Have they gotten rid of it? Well, time changes everything, Rupert. We mustn't yearn for the good old days like a couple of old coots. The plan still applies. We investigate all available scrumptious terribly-bad-probably-going-to-kill-you food before making our first choice."

Rupert nodded. He didn't care much for the method part of the plan. His idea was to hit the first amazing-smelling place they came to, order whatever it offered, and go on from there. He was so hungry that he was sure mud would taste delicious. Besides, it all smelled fantastic, it all smelled wonderfully of hot fat and burning sugar and fried meats. How could one choose? It was a hungry boy's paradise and apparently Uncle Henry's as well. He had the glazed look of a mad dog descending on the kill.

"Okay, okay," said Uncle Henry as they walked swiftly and purposefully about, checking out the food stands, looking at posted menus and at people sucking down giant ice cream cones and corn dogs.

"We mustn't be greedy! We mustn't be precipitate! OOOOO, I want one of *THOSE*! What the blazes is that?" asked Uncle Henry, rushing up to a man carrying a confection in a paper bowl and spooning it in as fast as he could.

"HEY, GET YOUR OWN!" shouted the man as Uncle Henry stuck his finger into the side of the man's bowl, scooped up some chocolate sauce, and tasted it.

"He's eating a funnel cake," said the man's wife with bewildered good manners. "And I'm eating a giant sausage sandwich. With mustard."

"Yes, yes," said Uncle Henry impatiently. "I *know* a giant sausage sandwich when I see it. It was the funnel cake I was interested in."

"You can get them over there," said the woman, pointing helpfully to a booth at the end of the park.

Uncle Henry took off like a shot with Rupert running behind.

"Is this okay, Rupert?" Uncle Henry asked, his voice

shaking with excitement. "I mean, I know I've *blown* the method. *Simply* jumped ship. There are dozens of food stands to check out still. But after I get one of those funnel cakes we can go back to the plan as previously laid out. Then we can make our next selection out of a well-ordered, numbered, and prioritized..."

"JUST GET ME SOME FOOD!" shouted Rupert, unable to contain himself as they once more traversed the park over the hot sand. "I'm starving to death and the smell of the food is making me *CRAZY!*"

"Right," said Uncle Henry, getting in line at the funnel cake stand. "You certainly are coming alive here. I don't know that I've ever heard you string so many words together, but no need to shout."

Rupert and Uncle Henry inched forward slowly in the line. It was a perfect day for the beach and it seemed all of New York, all of America, all of the *world* was at Coney Island and half of them were at the concession stands. But, finally, when Rupert thought he might faint from hunger and anticipation, they were at the head of the line. Rupert could hardly believe it. He wasn't only going to eat. He was going to eat one of those incredible confections. He hadn't eaten stomach-filling food like this since Christmas. He wondered if Uncle Henry would let him keep eating until he was as full as he had been then.

"Two funnel cakes please," said Uncle Henry,

chuckling with glee. "And two— What would you like to drink, Rupert?"

"Coke," said Rupert. He remembered it fondly from the bar at Zefferelli's. And he saw many people with icy sweating bottles of it drifting about.

"Right. Good choice, that will pair beautifully. And two Cokes, please," said Uncle Henry. "Ah, Rupert. This is going to be a treat. I've never had a funnel cake, but it looks wonderful."

"What do you want on it?" asked the concessionaire.

"EVERYTHING!" said Uncle Henry. "I want *the works*! And you, Rupert?"

Rupert didn't know what *the works* was but it sounded about right to him. "The works for me too!" he exclaimed joyfully.

Oh, he was warm and he would soon be fed! This time machine was the greatest thing ever. It was better than going to Zefferelli's! It was better than floating tables! What a day they were going to have. And then for a second he felt guilty because, really, Mrs. Rivers and the floating tables had been wonderful too. He didn't want to take anything away from that. But this was very very good and the food was more plentiful.

The concessionaire brought two paper bowls to the edge of the counter. The funnel cakes were covered in ice cream and every imaginable sauce—caramel and chocolate and hot fudge and marshmallow with nuts and sprinkles and candied cherries.

"Work of art if I do say so myself," said the concessionaire. "That'll be six bucks."

"Six dollars! That's outrageous!" said Uncle Henry. "This is the nineteen seventies. I'm positive these fair treats were much cheaper way back then."

"What are you talking about?" barked the concessionaire. "Way back *when?* Are you crazy?"

"Still," said Uncle Henry, ignoring him, "I suppose you only live once, eh, Rupert?"

He reached around to his back pants pocket for his wallet. Uncle Henry was frozen for a second, staring into space in consternation. Then he patted both back pockets, his front pockets, and, in desperation, his shirt pocket.

"Uh-oh," he said. He leaned down and whispered to Rupert, "No money." Then he straightened up and said, "Sir, we refuse to pay these prices! We are taking a stand. But if you'll just hand over the cakes, we'll leave without making a fuss."

"Get OUTTA here, freeloaders!" said the concessionaire. "You're lucky I don't call the cops! Who wants a couple of funnel cakes with the works?" he called down the line to the crowd.

Uncle Henry turned and walked away with as much dignity as he could muster. Rupert tripped along behind him as he headed toward the long strip of water past the trees.

As soon as they found an empty bench Uncle Henry pulled Rupert, who was still reeling from this turn of events, down to sit beside him.

"Bad news, boy," he said. "Left my wallet at home."

"YOU LEFT YOUR WALLET AT HOME?" Rupert could not help wailing in disappointment and, it must be admitted, a certain amount of exasperation.

"Hush. Well, I don't carry it around with me in the house. I put it in my pocket when I'm about to go out the front door, but we didn't *go* out the front door, did we, boy?"

Rupert shook his head miserably.

"No good crying over spilt milk. The question is, what can we do that doesn't require money? Hmmm. Let's see now. Can't go on rides, can't eat anything, not really dressed for the beach..."

Uncle Henry's face was all screwed up with concentration while Rupert sat, his stomach rumbling, and peeled off his sweatshirt and two of his shirts, tying them around his waist, for it was blazing hot on the bench in the sun. He really didn't care what they did until he had something in his stomach, for he was so hungry now he could hardly think straight.

"You know," Rupert mused out loud as they watched the swimmers going in and out of the water,

"I always thought the ocean would be bigger, somehow. I always thought it would have big waves and that you wouldn't be able to see the opposite shore."

"What do you mean? Of course it has big waves. Of course you can't see the opposite shore. That would be, oh, France or England or someplace," said Uncle Henry. "And it's not as if you can swim to those places from here." Then he looked more attentively at the beach and the water. "You're right, boy. You're on to something. Why, that's not the ocean at all."

"And what's that big ship thing with the wheel?" asked Rupert.

"That's . . . why that's a paddle wheeler. A *riverboat*," said Uncle Henry. "I don't believe we are where we thought we were. But we must be. The sign said CONEY ISLAND. There's food. There's a roller coaster. There's a beach. This is most vexing."

Uncle Henry leapt to his feet and put his hand on the arm of a young man who was walking by with his girlfriend. She was draped over his arm and staring at him in utter adoration.

"Listen, folks," said Uncle Henry. "Hate to intrude, but where are we exactly?"

The couple stopped and the young man looked at him as if he wasn't sure if Uncle Henry was kidding or not.

"What? You making fun of me or something?" he asked.

"No indeed, last thing I would do," said Uncle Henry, eyeing the young man's angry face and backing up a few feet.

"Well, then, are you stupid or something?" asked the young man.

"Yes, let's go with that," said Uncle Henry. "The thing is, that just doesn't look like the ocean to us." He pointed at the water. "Even if we squint."

"You *are* stupid," said the young man. "There's no ocean in Ohio."

"Everyone knows that," said the woman, squeezing the man's arm in admiration and batting her eyes.

"Ohio?" said Uncle Henry. "But Coney Island's in New York. On the Atlantic Ocean."

"Not this one, buddy. Hey," the man said, looking down at his girlfriend and smiling, "this idiot doesn't even know what state he's in."

"This is Coney Island park in Cincinnati," said the woman. "You know, Ohio?"

"Oh yes," said Uncle Henry, feigning comprehension. "*That* Coney Island. Well, lovely park. We plan to come here a lot in the future, eh, Rupert?"

But Rupert just stood with his mouth hanging open.

"But you can't," said the woman.

"Jeez, these guys really are clueless," said the young man in delight. "It's the park's last day. It closes after tonight."

"Yeah, it's a big deal," said the woman. "There's going to be fireworks and everything tonight."

"I see," said Uncle Henry, who had had enough of this know-it-all pair. "Well, yes, now that you mention it, I do remember reading about this park and how it was on Lake . . ."

"Jeez, I never met someone so stupid," said the young man wonderingly. "It's on the banks of the Ohio River, bud. Come on, babe, let's get out of here. This guy's loony tunes."

"He's just ignorant, Freddy," said the woman, smiling kindly at Uncle Henry, and they drifted off.

"Ah, that solves that. Now that they mention it, I knew something was wrong with the water. It isn't running perpendicular to the shore in the manner of oceans, but parallel to it. Let this be the deciding factor when determining ocean or river, Rupert. Let it be instructive—watch the direction in which the water flows. But who knew there were two Coney Islands? Well, you learn something every day. Explains the boardwalk situation. Not to mention why we could suddenly see across to France. Yuk yuk." Uncle Henry began chuckling wryly, but stopped when he caught a glimpse of Rupert's face.

Rupert had turned pale and was sitting on the bench shaking ever so slightly.

"Rupert, speak to me, what's the matter? Are you

going to faint again? As I recall, that seemed to be your special talent at Christmas."

"That couple?" said Rupert, swaying slightly in shock.

Uncle Henry nodded as the two of them watched the know-it-all pair make their way down the beach.

"They're my mom and dad."

FREDDY AND DELIA

DON'T BE ridiculous, Rupert," said Uncle Henry. "They're far too young to have a ten-year-old boy. They look to be teenagers themselves."

"Well, you said this was 1970-something," said Rupert.

Uncle Henry stopped and thought for a moment. "That's true. Yes, then that would be about right."

He flagged down a passing family who were looking for some place to sit to eat their giant bowls of funnel cake.

"You folks," said Uncle Henry. "You can have this bench if you tell us what year it is."

"1971," said the father.

"Rupert, get up and give the family your seat," said Uncle Henry.

Rupert stood up and the family spread out on the bench and began greedily lifting their funnel cake bowls, tilting them toward their mouths, and dripping melted ice cream and chocolate sauce down their fronts.

"Wow! That was an easy one," said one of the kids. "Do you have other questions? Will you give me something for telling you it's September? What else can we win?"

"Nothing. Game's over," said Uncle Henry. "And by the way, how do you like those funnel things?"

"Are you kidding, greatest invention on earth," said the mother.

"Except for the cotton candy dipped caramel apple burgers," said one of the boys. "They're even better."

"They don't make them anymore," said the mother. "Not since that man had a heart attack while eating one. It was in the newspaper. His family sued."

Rupert groaned involuntarily. He *would* be too late for the cotton candy dipped caramel apple burger. He'd never eaten any of those things singly except for the apple, but he had seen them all being eaten today by passersby and he felt all of them together must be heaven.

"Come along," said Uncle Henry irritably. "Don't ruin these nice folks' appetites by drooling on their shoes. And stop making that dying cow sound. How many times have I told you, if you must be a waif, be a cheerful waif."

"You've never told me that," said Rupert in some confusion as Uncle Henry pulled him along. "Where are we going now?"

"I thought it was obvious. We're going to follow your parents and look for our opportunity."

"Our opportunity for what?" asked Rupert. He had known his parents for nearly eleven years and he couldn't think what kind of opportunity they would ever afford anyone.

"To lift your dad's wallet."

"We're going to *steal* from my father?" asked Rupert in dismay.

"Nonsense, think of it as a loan," said Uncle Henry. "He's your father, for God's sake."

This sounded extremely dubious to Rupert. "What if they need the money?"

"So do we," said Uncle Henry decidedly.

"What if he sees me?" asked Rupert. "I don't think they noticed me before on the bench."

"Are you kidding? It's 1971. You haven't even been born yet. We'll steal his wallet and get some food and go on some rides and have a nice day and then we can go back to our own time and it will be like nothing ever happened. No harm, no foul."

"We can't do that!" said Rupert in alarm. "Our teacher read us a story by Ray Bradbury and these people go back in time just like we have and are supposed to touch nothing but they accidentally step on a butterfly and when they get back to their own time that one little accident has changed everything."

"That's *fiction*!" said Uncle Henry.

"But what if that *does* happen?"

"Well, I hate to tell you, Rupert, but I've already squished a mosquito that was biting me, so I guess I've changed the course of history already. In for a penny, in for a pound."

"Oh, I don't *like* this," said Rupert. "What if now we go back to our own time but we never were."

"Oh, buck up, don't you want a funnel cake?" asked Uncle Henry, still pulling Rupert along.

They found Rupert's parents standing in line for the roller coaster.

"Perfect," said Uncle Henry. "Your father's paying no attention to his pants pocket. This is going to be a piece of cake."

"Have you ever done this before?" asked Rupert.

"One or two times," said Uncle Henry vaguely. "And frankly, I'm surprised *you* haven't. You're the one without any money. Didn't this ever occur to you as a source of income?"

"*STEALING*?" squealed Rupert.

"Shush, do you want someone to sic the fuzz on us? Now, we just need to get up behind him."

"We can't do that because they're not going to let us in line without tickets," said Rupert. "Let's just go home."

"Let's *just go home*?" mimicked Uncle Henry in disbelief. "You *are* a spineless little jellyfish, aren't you?

What are they making children out of these days? Rupert, I hate to say it, but you're a total washout as a partner in crime."

"I don't want to be your partner in crime," wailed Rupert. "I don't want to steal from my own father."

"He's not your father *yet*," said Uncle Henry. "Try to think of it that way. Or here's another way—if he's your father, it isn't stealing, it's just borrowing from the family coffers."

"I don't want to borrow from a bunch of dead persons, that's even worse!" cried Rupert.

This stumped Uncle Henry for a moment until a light went on and he said, "That's *coffers*, not *coffins*, you little ignoramus. I thought you were the genius child. Really, Rupert, I don't see how you won all those prizes at Christmas. I really don't."

"I had something to eat that day," said Rupert miserably.

"Right. Well, we're working on that. You have had one good insight. You were right when you said we can't get behind your father without tickets for the ride. Hmmm, what to do, what to do?"

As Uncle Henry said this he brushed up against a bunch of people standing in a knot trying to decide which ride to choose. One of them was trailing a long string of tickets but didn't seem to be paying much attention to them.

"Come on," Uncle Henry whispered to Rupert. "Our ship has come in!"

And to Rupert's astonishment Uncle Henry sidled up and, before Rupert could say anything, ripped off half a dozen tickets from the man's string. Then he pulled Rupert to the ticket taker at the roller coaster ride.

Once in line, Uncle Henry moved them slowly forward, cutting in front of everyone by saying, "Excuse us, excuse us, this young man's gotten separated from his family! Poor fellow is about to cry!" He pinched Rupert surreptitiously and whispered, "Cry, Rupert!"

"I will not!" Rupert whispered back.

In this way they slowly moved up the line. No one seemed to really mind. Uncle Henry was dressed in his usual impeccable silk polo shirt and chinos with his rich person's haircut and penny loafers with no socks. His appearance fairly screamed I HAVE A LOT OF MONEY, GET OUT OF MY WAY! He was not the sort of person anyone would suspect of lying or trying to cut ahead in line without a sound reason. And Rupert was just a pathetic-looking child. The sun was hot and people were full of funnel cakes and various confections and had no energy to argue anyway. Before they knew it, Uncle Henry and Rupert were standing right behind Rupert's dad.

"Oh, Freddy, do you really think we should do

this?" asked Rupert's mom. "I'm scared. I've never been on a roller coaster."

"Delia, don't worry, I'll hold you tight."

"Oh, would you, Freddy?" asked Rupert's mom. "I think I might feel safer if you would."

"Oh yuck," said Uncle Henry. But Rupert was mesmerized. He had never heard his parents talk to each other this way before. He had never heard them do anything but snipe at each other.

"I'm so lucky I met you here," said Rupert's mom. "I almost didn't come to Coney Island. I had to get talked into it by my girlfriends, and, say, speaking of them, I oughta let them know where I am. I was supposed to spend the day with *them*."

"Yeah, well, they'll figure it out," said Freddy. "So where did you all come from?"

"Well, I used to live in Kentucky. I just moved to Steelville this summer when I graduated high school. My family wanted me to stay in Kentucky, but what was there for me? I was the first person in my family to graduate high school and I said I wasn't wasting my diploma in those hills. I wanted to make something of myself. One of my girlfriends said she was going to Steelville because she heard the steelworks there was hiring, so I went along. It's been real different and exciting too, Freddy."

"Huh," said Freddy. "That's cool."

"Where are you from, Freddy?"

"Well, that's kind of the coincidence. I come from Kentucky too. But I moved to Cincinnati."

"Gee, where in Kentucky? I'm from Pikeville."

"Oh, here and there. You know."

"Did you graduate this year too?

"Sort of," said Freddy.

"Whaddya do here in Cincinnati?" asked Rupert's mom. "I bet you found a better job than me."

"Oh, this and that," said Freddy. "What do you do, anyway?"

"Well, when I got to the steelworks it was kind of bad luck because the only job they said they had for me was cleaning the offices, but, you know, I figure it's a starter job and it won't be long before I've got something much better. I hear they really move you up fast at the steelworks. You know, once you get your foot in the door. I'm going to be management someday, Freddy, and I'm going to get a suit and a pair of real crocodile pumps and I'm going to go home to Kentucky and walk up and down Main Street in 'em so everyone can see."

"Well, I bet there's more jobs in Cincinnati than Steelville," observed Rupert's dad sagely. "Because it's, you know, much bigger."

"Oh, you bet, but Cincinnati would be *too* big for me. I was looking at it when we drove in and I thought, jeez, I'd get *lost* here. But I bet you don't get lost, do you?"

"Yeah, not much," said Freddy.

"Do you like it a lot here, Freddy?"

"I dunno. Not so much maybe. It doesn't have as much going for it as I thought it would."

"Well, there's supposed to be lots of jobs coming up in Steelville. Everybody's talking about it. How they'll get a better job soon. Maybe you want to come try to get a job at the steelworks."

"Yeah, maybe. I don't know. I got maybe an iron or two in the fire. I would hate to, you know, miss out on those."

"Yeah, I get it, but then maybe we could see each other more." Rupert's mother blushed.

"Well, hey, I got an idea. Why don't you tell those friends of yours that I'll give you a ride home after the fireworks tonight? I got a real cool Trans Am I'm working on. It only broke down once on the way here."

"Gee, do you know all about cars too, Freddy?"

"Yeah, pretty much everything there is."

"I always admire a guy who knows about cars," said Delia, and squeezed his arm again.

While they were chatting and Rupert was listening enthralled, Uncle Henry was inching his hand closer and closer to Rupert's dad's back pocket. His fingers were poised right over the bulging wallet when Freddy leaned back, slid both his hands into his back pockets and stretched. Uncle Henry barely had time to snatch his own hand out of the way.

"NO!" whispered Uncle Henry ferociously. "NO! I was *this* close."

"Now what?" Rupert whispered back.

But at that moment the roller coaster stopped and people began exiting. The ticket taker started to put the new crowd on.

"We'll just have to wait until we sit next to him in the roller coaster car. They sit you four across," said Uncle Henry. "I'll make sure to maneuver it so I sit next to him. During the ride when he's screaming in terror, I'll lift the wallet."

"But he'll be *sitting* on it," said Rupert.

"I'll figure out something," muttered Uncle Henry as they shuffled forward. To their dismay, Rupert's parents were seated with the couple who stood in front of them in line instead.

"No, no, no," said Uncle Henry as they were escorted to seats behind Rupert's parents. He bounced up and down in his seat, getting frowns from the couple seated next to them who wanted to maneuver the safety bar down over the four of them, but Uncle Henry's jumping prohibited it.

"I'm sorry," said Uncle Henry, tapping the man sitting next to Freddy on the shoulder. "But you are in our seats. Let's all get up and switch."

"Whah?" said the man, turning around and looking at Uncle Henry as if he were crazy.

"You're sitting where we meant to sit," said Uncle Henry with a show of extreme patience.

"Get outta here!" said the man, turning back to face the front again.

"Can you just let us put the bar down? They're about to start the ride," said the woman sitting next to Uncle Henry politely. She glanced nervously at the man running the roller coaster. He had seated everyone and was headed back to the controls.

"Yeah, sit down and pipe down," said the man sitting next to Freddy. "Or we'll have you put off!"

"Oh, I very much doubt that, young man," said Uncle Henry. "I own half of Steelville."

"Who cares?" said the man. "This is Cincinnati."

"Hey," said Freddy, turning around and addressing Uncle Henry. "Do you have anything to do with jobs at the steelworks?"

"I do, indeed, my fine fellow. And what is your name?" asked Uncle Henry.

"Freddy Brown," said Rupert's father.

"Well, I'll have to see some I.D. to corroborate that," said Uncle Henry.

"They're starting the ride!" said the woman sitting next to Uncle Henry. "We've got to put the bar down *now*! Do you want to fall out of this thing?"

"Not especially," said Uncle Henry. "But this will only take a second. If you could just get your wallet out, Mr. Brown? And pass it to me? I'll get your I.D. out myself and return it to you at the end of the ride."

"Hey," said Rupert's mom, turning around and looking at Uncle Henry. "You're the guy from earlier. The one who didn't know what state he was in. Freddy, this guy doesn't own half of Steelville. He's a flake."

"Jeez, you're right, Delia, good call. I should've known. I never get a break." Rupert's dad's face fell and he squirmed back around to face forward.

The woman sitting next to Uncle Henry pushed him down properly in his seat, grabbed the safety bar, and yanked it in front of the four of them, and the car began its slow climb.

"Listen, Mac," called Rupert's dad over his shoulder. "I catch you hassling me or my girlfriend again and you'll be sorry!"

"Oh," said Delia, fluttering. "Am I really your girlfriend already, Freddy?"

But before Freddy could answer, the cars had dropped and they all stopped talking and started screaming instead.

Rupert forgot about everything but the sensation of the air rushing past him and the dizzying sense that he was no longer upright. Around in a horrible upside-down loop they flew. He thought he might throw up but before he could, the car slowed down again and he opened his eyes to find them rolling gradually to a stop on level ground at the ride's exit.

"Well," Uncle Henry said as they walked shakily off the car and made their way to a nearby bench where they both put their heads down between their knees. "I planned to lift his wallet when they got up to leave but I was feeling a bit shaky there, Rupert, boy. It's been a long time since I've been on a roller coaster. If I ever suggest going on one of those death machines again, please do dissuade me."

"So it was a bust," said Rupert from his upside-down position.

"Not entirely," said Uncle Henry, sitting up again. "We've still got four tickets. Come on, there they are, walking down the midway. Let's follow them. We're sure to get another opportunity."

Uncle Henry and Rupert managed to get behind Rupert's parents as they stood in line for the shooting gallery.

"Are you going to win me something, Freddy?" asked Delia.

"Yeah, I'm pretty good with a gun," said Freddy. "I've been hunting squirrels since I was six. And listen, we can get some eats and take them down to the river and find a good spot for the fireworks."

"Oh, Freddy, that would be divine," said Delia. "You have the best ideas of anyone I ever met."

"Yeah, I think my ideas are really, like, one of my best traits. My last girlfriend always said, you're gonna make a million bucks with those ideas, Freddy."

"Oh, I believe you are," said Delia, looking up at him with shining eyes.

Uncle Henry almost had his hand in Freddy's pocket when Freddy reached around to take out his wallet.

"Darn it!" said Uncle Henry. "The kid's got radar."

"*YOU* again!" said Freddy, as his hand brushed Uncle Henry's retreating fingers. "Are you *following* us?"

"Oh, Freddy, I think you're right. I think they *are* following us," said Delia, clutching his arm. "Do you think they're criminals? Do you think they're here to pick our pockets?"

"How do I know? It's not like I've been in jail maybe or prison for, like, just a short time for something I hardly even did where I could meet guys like that," said Freddy indignantly.

Meanwhile Uncle Henry had grabbed the opportunity to pull Rupert back into the crowd, saying, "Cheese it, they made us."

They quickly wound their way through the crowd, getting lost in it.

"Now what?" asked Rupert when they stopped to catch their breath.

"A Rivers never gives up," said Uncle Henry. "Come on, we don't have food or money but we still have four tickets left. Let's go on a couple of rides and give your parents some space. Then we can find them again sometime before the fireworks start."

"Maybe we should just get in the time machine and go home," said Rupert. He was getting tired and he never wanted to take his father's wallet to begin with. He had never seen his parents having such a good time and he felt the right thing to do was to leave them alone to enjoy it.

"I'm not departing this place until I get a funnel cake," said Uncle Henry.

"Okay," said Rupert. "But there're so many rides. Which one do you want to go on? I don't want to be upside down again."

"Don't worry," said Uncle Henry. "I have given the matter some thought and have formulated a comprehensive plan."

Uncle Henry's plan for picking rides was pretty much the same plan he had had for picking food. It involved surveying all the rides and then making a careful list of rides they most wanted to go on. This took some time but, except for Rupert's ever-gnawing hunger and the wonderful torturous smells of the food, he enjoyed it. The crowds alone were fun to watch. And the unaccustomed preponderance of hot pink and baby blue. Sticks of hot pink and baby blue cotton candy drifted by in the sweaty hands of fairgoers. Hot pink and baby blue stuffed animals and balloons were held aloft. Rupert realized that just the newness of a place with such different predominant colors was wonderful. Newness was a great thing, he decided. It somehow woke you up.

The only ride Rupert saw that he wanted to go on was the merry-go-round. But Uncle Henry seemed to have forgotten his terror on the roller coaster and how he had said he would never step foot on such a death machine again, and now he wanted to go on the octopus and the twister, the Tilt-A-Whirl, and a horrible thing that looked like a spinning cage. In the end, they compromised on the merry-go-round for Rupert and the Ferris wheel for Uncle Henry.

Rupert enjoyed the merry-go-round even though Uncle Henry kept sullenly muttering, "It's nothing like a real horse. Why do they bother? You can't even canter them. This posting trot is getting tedious. And, I mean, pink and blue ponies? It's nauseating. The polo club would vomit if they saw this."

Uncle Henry hadn't eaten in a while either and unlike Rupert he wasn't used to this. He could not even put his finger on the unusual sensations he was feeling.

All he knew was that he was feeling cranky and there was a peculiar emptiness to his stomach. The mothers he accosted with advice about equitation were moving one by one to the other side of the merry-go-round until Rupert and Uncle Henry were quite alone.

Rupert sighed. He wondered if Uncle Henry was going to cause them to be put off the ride, but after a bit Uncle Henry quieted down and looked sullenly out as round and round they went. The afternoon had faded into evening and lights were coming on all over the park as the sun began to go down over the river, leaving red and orange streaks in the roiling water.

"It may almost be time for fireworks," said Uncle Henry as they lined up for the Ferris wheel. "It is my experience that they shoot them off as soon as the sun sets."

"Maybe we should skip the Ferris wheel and go down to the riverbank to find a place to sit and watch them," said Rupert, eyeing the enormous wheel nervously.

"We've time. I'm sure we've time, and besides, it's the perfect way to see where your parents have gotten to. We'll be able to survey the whole park from the top."

Rupert knew it was useless to argue with Uncle Henry, so with trepidation he got on the Ferris wheel next to him. But as soon as it started to go up he realized that he hated this almost *more* than the roller coaster.

It not only took you high up, the car swung back and forth and—oh, horror—*stopped* at the very top.

"Oh no, oh no, oh no," chanted Rupert, clinging to the safety bar with white knuckles. "Let us down. Let us down. There must be something wrong! Some reason it has stopped. We'll be killed!"

"Oh, get a grip. These things are always stopping," said Uncle Henry, evidently enjoying himself. "Let's see if we can make it really rock."

"Please no," pleaded Rupert. His eyes were firmly shut.

"AHA!" screamed Uncle Henry suddenly.

"AM I GOING TO DIE?" screamed Rupert back.

"No, you idiot. Who screams AHA when announcing imminent death? Surely you would scream, OHMYGOD! or IVEALWAYSLOVEDYOU or ITWASI-WHODROPPEDYOURTOOTHBRUSHINTHETOILET! No, you twit, it's your parents! I can see them. For heaven's sake, open your eyes and quickly take a look. We're moving again and soon we'll be too low to clock them. Take note, they're to the right of the corn dog stand and under that big tree."

Rupert opened his eyes and gasped. He could see the whole park, not that he wanted to. He looked where Uncle Henry was pointing until he found his parents. They were under a tree by the riverbank, kissing as if their whole lives depended on it.

"My goodness," chuckled Uncle Henry.

Rupert was embarrassed but also fascinated. It had never occurred to him that his parents had ever felt this way about each other or done things like kiss passionately under a tree on a soft September evening.

"Come on, we've got to get off," Rupert said when they reached the bottom, but of course they couldn't get off. The Ferris wheel went down but then backward and up they went again. Rupert had to endure three more loops. It was agonizing at first, but Rupert kept his eyes open this time and forgot about his fears in order to catch a glimpse of his parents again. And so he also saw the throngs of people moving in streams between food stands and rides. And the stars coming out in the sky. The twinkling lights of the riverboats and the moon now rising full and orange above it all. And every time they reached the top he saw his parents, their arms around each other as if holding on for dear life in the swiftly moving, always changing, mutable, morphable universe.

By the time the Ferris wheel had stopped, loud speakers were announcing that the fireworks display was about to begin.

People began to drift in that direction like tributaries trickling to the river.

"Come on!" urged Uncle Henry, grabbing Rupert's hand, and together they ran to the riverbank, dodging around the throngs of people heading the same way.

The first firework had already gone off by the time they settled on the ground behind the tree underneath which lay Rupert's parents.

"I'm really starving," said Uncle Henry. "If we can't get your dad's wallet I say we go after someone else's. Come to think of it, I have no idea now why I've been so focused on only one wallet. Sheer idiocy. Tunnel vision. There's hundreds of wallets here. Any one will do. It's completely justified. People shouldn't starve. Or be deprived of funnel cake. *Completely* justified. And, after all, soon we will be returning to our own time and it will be as if we've never been here, so what difference does it make? Who ends up with the money for funnel cake is, after all, a rather random thing anyway, isn't it? I mean, it's not as if they are more deserving than we are. And look, no one is paying any attention, they're all looking up at the fireworks. Oh look, look, we caught a break, your dad is lying on his side, I've got a real good shot at getting into his pants pocket. Just watch me. Funnel cake is seconds away, boy."

Uncle Henry inched his way along the ground on his belly while fireworks went off above and the crowd oohed and aahed.

"Oh, Freddy, it's so beautiful," sighed Delia. "It's the most beautiful thing I've ever seen."

"I meant what I said before, you know . . . What's your name again?"

153

"Delia."

"Right, Delia, you're, like, my girlfriend now," said Freddy. "Maybe I *will* move to Steelville. I mean, it's not like Cincinnati. It won't have the same kind of opportunities that a guy like me deserves, but I gotta a feeling about us, Delia."

"You do, Freddy?"

"Sure, I do."

"'Cause I gotta a feeling about us, too, Freddy," said Delia in almost a whisper. "I've had a lot of boyfriends but I never felt this way about a guy before. Right off the bat, you know? Gosh, my own parents didn't stay together; I didn't even much know my dad ever. And my mom—I don't remember her ever being happy. She was sad the whole time I was growing up and I thought, you know, she just never had anyone. That was why she was so sad. And growing up watching her being sad all the time, I never wanted that for me. I never wanted to be lonely. I always thought, you know, if I could find the right person, then I could have a happy life. That's what I think. If you're with the right person who makes you happy, you can be happy forever, Freddy. I believe that. Do you believe that, Freddy?"

"Yeah, Delia," said Freddy, "I never talked to anyone like this before. But yeah, I do. I think I feel the same. I think I never met no one like you before. I feel, I don't know, different. Like maybe life's not such a rough deal after all. Like maybe you're the good thing that's going to happen to me in my life. I've been waiting for a good thing to happen. I always thought I was special, but nothin' special ever happens for me. But now I think maybe you're it."

"Oh, Freddy," whispered Delia, turning her face up to kiss him. "No one ever said anything like that to me before."

Delia sat up again and Freddy sat up next to her and her hand found Freddy's and they tilted their heads up to the fireworks. It was if they could see all of their young lives and ambitions and dreams and hopes exploding over their heads above them. Freddy leaned in closer now for a kiss but it wasn't like the passionate kisses they'd shared earlier, it was softer, more innocent, it was what he wished he could have been if things had started out differently for him. Afterward Delia dropped her head gently on his shoulder, and they sat like that in one perfect moment in the warm dark.

Uncle Henry was still scooting toward them, dodging out of sight every time Freddy's angle changed, when suddenly he stopped.

"What's that sound?" he asked, turning to Rupert in sudden panic.

Rupert was startled out of the trance he had fallen into listening to his young parents on the day they met, and he turned and said, "Huh? Oh, that's a truck coming down the dirt road. It's a..." His eyes strained to see in the dark.

"What kind of a truck?" asked Uncle Henry in alarm.

"A garbage truck," said Rupert unconcernedly.

But suddenly the meaning of this pierced through Rupert's trance and he leapt up. Uncle Henry was already on his feet and running.

The time machine!

Uncle Henry and Rupert shoved their way through the packed crowd on the riverbank with people saying irritably, "Hey, you two, quit shoving!" But they ignored everyone in their desperation to get to the hot dog stand. When they finally reached it, panting and sweating, they found all the boxes gone.

"You, garbage guys!" said Uncle Henry, chasing behind the truck and panting so heavily he could hardly speak. "Where are the boxes that were behind that stand over there?"

"Whuh?" asked the garbageman, stopping the truck.

"The boxes that were just here! The boxes?"

"What do you mean? They're in the truck, where else?"

"NO! OH NO!" shouted Uncle Henry. "Well, you're going to have to empty the truck back out. One of them was there by mistake. I need it. I can't go home without it."

"What are you talking about?" said the garbageman. "Look, there's empty cartons behind all the stands. Why don't you just go get yourself another box?"

"No, no, I don't want just any box, I want a particular one," said Uncle Henry. "It had something special in it."

"Well, it's gone now," said the garbageman. "This truck eats up anything we put in it. It crushes and mashes and packs it down. Your special box is *gone,* guy. Sorry." And he leapt onto the truck and moved on.

Uncle Henry and Rupert looked at each other, their faces pale.

"This is terrible," said Rupert. "Are we stuck here? But what will happen to us? How can we be at all if we haven't been born yet?"

"Well, you haven't been born; I'm about thirty by now," said Uncle Henry.

"But that's *worse,*" said Rupert. "That means there's another one of you running around. And I don't want to stay here. We don't have a home or anything. What are we going to do?"

"I don't know," said Uncle Henry. "Let me think."

"Maybe you could invent another time machine," said Rupert.

"Are you kidding me? I don't know how I invented the first one," said Uncle Henry. "Now, it might not be that bad. I mean, maybe we just have to get back to Steelville. After all, back in 1971 I was living in the same house as I am now. We just go there and I say you are moving in and..."

"No, that's a terrible idea!" said Rupert. "There will be two of you. What happens when you're both in the room at once? Which one will YOU be?"

"We could tell people we're twins."

"You can't be twins if one of you is older than the other."

"Good thinking, Rupert. Well, I could be my younger self's mentor. Mentors are always hanging around force-feeding people advice. I rather like the idea of myself in that role."

"I think they would remember that there didn't used to be a mentor hanging around that looked just like your younger self only older."

"Would they? Do you really think people pay so much attention? Anyway, here's another idea. Maybe the younger self disappeared when the older self appeared. After all, we don't really know how all this works. Maybe only one version of yourself ever exists at any one time."

"Oh, sure, that would be just great—explaining to them how you'd suddenly aged so much. And what about me? How can I be ten if my mother hasn't even given birth to me yet?"

"Don't fret so, Rupert. Time is a tricky thing, so

let us leave the details to the physicists with their big brains. It is enough that at least we know where to find a roof over our heads."

"*Argh,*" said Rupert, pulling at his hair. "You have a nice house but I don't want to *live* in it. I want my own home."

"Really?" said Uncle Henry. "Extraordinary. It can't be as nice as my home. I would have thought you'd have leapt at the chance."

"NO, I just want my own life!" Rupert began to bellow in panicked exasperation when a garbage truck ambled by, going from stand to stand collecting trash. "Wait a second! Look at where the truck is going *next*."

"So?" said Uncle Henry.

"It's *another* hot dog stand. Uncle Henry, I don't think this is where we put the box after all. I think it was at that *other* stand over there, closer to the gate."

Uncle Henry looked to the gate. "I believe you're... holy moly, Rupert! Run. Run. The truck is almost there."

Uncle Henry ran fast. He was old but he had long legs. Rupert was young but he had short legs. They were both in a panic. They reached the stand together just as the garbageman stepped out of his truck to collect the boxes.

"WAIT!" yelled Uncle Henry, rapidly throwing the pile of hot dog boxes over his shoulder one by one as he frantically searched for the time machine.

"Hey, stop it, you're making a mess," yelled the garbage guy. "I don't want to be collecting all those boxes from..."

But before he could finish Uncle Henry cried, "EUREKA! We got it, boy! We got it! Now quick! Before something else happens!"

Uncle Henry opened out the box and jumped in, followed by Rupert. Before Uncle Henry could begin his arm-waving theatrics, there was a whizzing and whirring sound, and the next thing they knew they were sitting on the attic floor of the Riverses' house.

"Ha!" said Uncle Henry in triumph. "Ha!"

Then they were both so exhausted they could think of nothing else to say. Rupert untied his shirts and sweatshirt and put them back on. Once they got their breath, they crept down the stairs. The Rivers family could be seen sitting in the dining room eating.

"Well, I suspect you're anxious to be off to your own dinner. Mustn't keep you," said Uncle Henry dismissively, practically pushing Rupert to the door. For truth be told, Uncle Henry was glad to be home and glad that it was no longer 1971. Glad that he didn't have to introduce a new person into his household and more than glad that he would never again have to wear paisley.

"Right," said Rupert. "Well, thank you. I've had a lovely time."

"Oh, it was nothing," said Uncle Henry, gently shoving him out the door.

Suddenly they were both embarrassed and self-conscious for reasons that were hard to explain. As if they were two strangers finding themselves having shared an experience too chummy for their comfort.

"Well, good-bye. Have a coat?" asked Uncle Henry distractedly, pushing the button by the front door that opened the gate. It was clear he wanted his supper and also that he'd forgotten Rupert didn't own a coat.

"No, just this," said Rupert, fingering his worn sweatshirt. "Well, good-bye and thanks again."

"Think nothing of it." Uncle Henry closed the door and Rupert trotted down the walkway through the freshly falling snow, shivering madly after the summer night he had just left. He was almost at the gate when Uncle Henry opened the door again and ran tearing up to him. Rupert had a sudden hope he was there to give him a sandwich or even a dinner roll, but instead Uncle Henry leaned in and whispered quickly, "I lied. It wasn't the Christmas pudding I felt bad about. It was the prizes. I felt bad about the prizes. Now I've broken my own rule. But I don't care."

And without another word, he ran swiftly back to the house.

Rupert watched after him in surprise for a moment and then trudged on home.

When he got to the front door his mother was just coming in from her job cleaning the offices at the steelworks. His father was lying on the couch, where he had lain all day watching TV.

"Have you got supper started?" Rupert's mother barked at his father.

"Nah, I didn't have time," said Rupert's father, and laughed.

"Where have *you* been?" Rupert's mother asked Rupert.

"Oh, just out," said Rupert, because he couldn't think of a quick-enough lie.

Rupert's mother gave Rupert a strange look. Then for a second her eyes went far away as if remembering something, and her face softened before rehardening again, and she said nothing but kicked her way through the clutter to the kitchen to begin the evening meal.

AUNT HAZELNUT'S JEWELS

ALL WEEK following the trip to Coney Island, Rupert sat in class daydreaming about the time machine. Perhaps by now Uncle Henry had recommended fiddling with it so they could control where they went. It seemed logical to Rupert that anyone who could make a time machine out of a plain cardboard box could figure out how to tweak it to take it where he wanted.

Rupert kept thinking of places for them to go. Places with *food*, places with *heat*. He spent more time daydreaming about those two things than he did about exotic locations and adventures. He had no desire to go anywhere cold or spartan; he'd love to see penguins, for example, but Antarctica was right *out*. Perhaps they could go to a tropical island, ripe with pineapples and coconuts and breadfruit. He had read about breadfruit—was it really bread that grew as fruit?—and had always wanted to try it. Or perhaps they could go to a great banquet in medieval times where they would cram their mouths with roasted meat in front of a roaring fire. Or maybe back to the 1950s to a Pillsbury Bake-Off where they could be the judges and go from table to table tasting all the cakes. His teacher had told the class how her grandmother had done this and Rupert had thought, yeah, those were the good old days.

Rupert walked super slowly past the Riverses' house every day on his way home from school. He tried to spot the periscope. Each day he was sure that a hand would come poking out of the hedge, grab him, and pull him through. But as day after day passed and there was no sign of Uncle Henry and his periscope, Rupert became disgruntled. Hadn't Uncle Henry had *fun* with him? Surely Uncle Henry didn't want to go on adventures alone when he could have Rupert along? Perhaps Uncle Henry felt that he had made up for whatever guilt he'd carried regarding Christmas and the prizes and had moved on. This was a depressing thought. Somehow Rupert felt a strange rapport with Uncle Henry after sharing the time machine's maiden voyage. He was deflated to think that Uncle Henry might not have felt the same.

When two weeks passed and Uncle Henry made no attempt to contact him, Rupert, out of desperation, flagged down Turgid in the hall before school started.

"I don't know if you remember me?" asked Rupert shyly.

"Oh yes," said Turgid. "You're Rudy, aren't you? From Christmas?"

Rupert couldn't believe that Turgid didn't even remember his name. They'd spent *Christmas* together! He, Rupert, must be the least memorable person on the face of the earth!

"Yes, I, I just wanted to ask how your Uncle Henry is? Not sick or anything, is he?"

"Sick? No, he's just as usual, thank you," said Turgid, looking puzzled.

"I mean, he's still *around,* isn't he?" asked Rupert, blushing. It had occurred to him as a last scenario that Uncle Henry had time traveled somewhere, gotten himself stuck there, and his family hadn't yet noticed.

"Yes, of course," said Turgid.

"Turns up every night for dinner?"

"Why wouldn't he?" asked Turgid.

"Right. Just...checking," said Rupert. Now he really was in despair.

"Very good. Very...considerate of you," said Turgid, and walked away shaking his head.

Rupert could hear one of Turgid's friends asking, "What are you doing talking to one of those weirdo Browns?"

"Oh, Rudy? He's all right. Had him over for Christmas. Not exactly our idea, but he kept fainting so, you know, we were obligated to keep him around until he recovered, and really he wasn't so bad, a little rough around the edges..." and their voices trailed off as they went down the hall.

Rupert, standing there watching them depart, blushed even deeper. Now it would be all over the school, the thing he had tried to avoid—everyone would say that he was a charity case. That he'd been invited to dinner not because anyone wanted to eat with him but because they felt sorry for him. But that really wasn't how it had happened at all, was it? They were the ones whose gate had caught him up and shocked him. Then Turgid had insisted he stay. He hadn't *asked* to stay. And what did Turgid mean by "rough around the edges"? What had Rupert done that was rough? And now he supposed he had to face facts: Uncle Henry was taking him on no more time-travel trips. The one had been the one and only. There would not be a series of madcap adventures together.

When he went on his adventure with Mrs. Rivers and then Uncle Henry he had thought, *Ah, now the exciting part of my life has begun!* He thought things were just getting going. He could not believe it was over so soon and from now on life would just grind on.

And yet it did for a time. January blizzards set in followed by February's ice storms until Rupert began to feel like an icicle himself, never thawing, always slightly blue.

Then, to cap it all off, his least favorite day of the year arrived: Valentine's Day. Every poor child in school dreaded Valentine's Day.

At Rupert's school the children decorated valentine mailboxes which they made out of shoe boxes. The children were supposed to bring a shoebox from home, but of course for the poor children this was often a difficulty and so the teachers always brought in a few for these children. This was the first humiliation.

Each child had to give every other child in his class a valentine. Most of the children's parents took them valentine shopping and they bought boxes of little cards with cartoon or movie or TV figures on them. Then the children spent part of the day in class printing names and sometimes messages on cards and delivering them.

The poor children usually arrived on Valentine's Day without any cards. This was addressed thoughtfully by the teachers, who put out construction paper and felt pens and crayons and glue and glitter and lace and stickers and let these children make their valentines during silent reading time. But although this was kindly intended, all it did was draw attention to the children who could not afford valentines, for they were the only ones laboring away, covered in glue and stickers.

Few children were unkind to those who couldn't buy their valentines, but there were always some who sniggered and teased when the teacher wasn't looking. And even if there hadn't been, to spend time making valentines—especially when you weren't, as Rupert wasn't, very good with your hands—was utter torture. Rupert always made a mess of his desk, with glue and glitter everywhere. He had once tried to cut out plain hearts, but the teacher had come by and said, *Now, now, we can do better than* this, *surely?* And heaped glitter and art supplies on Rupert's desk while the girls sitting around him looked politely away. All Rupert wanted to do on Valentine's Day was crawl under his desk and die, but, of course, no one let him do that either.

The great saving grace of Valentine's Day was that Rupert could count on getting something to eat because the day always ended in a class party. Any child could bring treats for the class as long as they brought enough for everyone. There was an excited atmosphere before school started as mothers dropped off bright pink cupcakes or heart-shaped cookies. And for once it didn't matter if people didn't like the Browns. Rules were rules and the booty was divided evenly. The food wasn't served until all the valentines had been delivered, but, thought Rupert, at least there was *that* to look forward to after the humiliation of making his valentines and having to go around with glue in his hair.

This year in Rupert's class there were three children having to make their valentines. Rupert had gotten

himself enough art supplies in order to look industri-
ous from the table where they'd been set out, but not so
many that he had to spend more time and make more of
a mess than necessary. He was busily putting glue and
glitter down on a heart and sniffing the wonderful smells
of cupcakes and icing and sugar coming from the front
of the room when the door of the classroom suddenly
opened with a blast of air and everyone looked up. They
expected to see the principal, who often peeked into
classrooms on special days, but instead they saw a tall,
imposing woman with a large hooked nose and a mass of
unruly red curls and a bright red lipsticked mouth. She
was wearing a mink stole and very high heels.

It was Aunt Hazelnut!

She must have come to the wrong classroom, thought
Rupert. *Turgid's grade six classroom was next door.*

Rupert's teacher obviously thought the same, for
she said, "Mrs. Rivers, are you looking for Turgid,
perhaps?"

Everyone in town knew all the Riverses. They were
celebrities in Steelville. Their clothes and their history
and their cars and their manner bespoke a position well
above everyone else. Even above the people in the other
six mansions.

"No," said Aunt Hazelnut. "I want..." And she
looked wildly around the room for a second before her
eyes settled on Rupert. "HIM!"

"Him?" echoed the teacher, looking to where Aunt Hazelnut was pointing but obviously not quite believing her eyes.

"Yes. HIM!" repeated Aunt Hazelnut.

"Rupert?" said the teacher, looking worried. Then she whispered to Aunt Hazelnut, but loud enough for Rupert to hear, "He hasn't stolen your cat, has he?"

"Don't be ridiculous," said Aunt Hazelnut. "What would I be doing with a cat? No, I want him right now. Please get him ready."

"Oh," said the teacher at a loss. "Has Mrs. Brown sent you to fetch him for some reason?"

"Mrs. Brown? I know no Mrs. Brown," said Aunt Hazelnut in the same imperious tone.

"Rupert's mother," said the teacher. "Or perhaps Mr. Brown?"

"Nobody sends me to fetch anything, young lady," said Aunt Hazelnut.

Rupert was amazed to hear his teacher referred to as young. He had never thought of his teacher as young, but he supposed she was, compared to Aunt Hazelnut.

"Yes, well, do you have a signed permission letter?" asked the teacher, pulling a file out of a drawer and going through it. "You know you have to be on a list of approved people to pick up a child. The parent has to provide these names at the beginning of the year. I just ask because Mrs. Brown didn't provide any names.

Not that I recall. Let me just see now, I can't, you know, release a child unless a person is on the list..."

The teacher continued to flip through the file nervously, not wanting to keep a Rivers waiting. While she was doing so Aunt Hazelnut marched over to Rupert's desk, picked up a crayon and a piece of red construction paper, and scrawled something. Then she brought it up to the teacher's desk.

"Here, will this do?"

The teacher took the piece of paper and read it out loud: "I hereby give my permission for Hazelnut Rivers to collect my son Rupert. Signed The Browns. Both Mrs. and Mr."

The teacher frowned. "I see," she said. She paused timorously. "Did you, uh, just now write this yourself?"

"How *DARE* you!" said Aunt Hazelnut. "What are you *IMPLYING*?"

"Well, uh, the thing is," said the teacher nervously, not knowing where to go with this next.

"Shall I just see the principal about this then?" asked Aunt Hazelnut.

"Oh, please do," said the teacher in relief, more than happy to pass the buck.

"I'll take Rupert with me, shall I?" said Aunt Hazelnut. "For expediency."

"Oh," said the teacher. "Take him out of the classroom?"

"You don't seriously believe I intend to kidnap him, do you?" asked Aunt Hazelnut. "A *RIVERS*?"

"No, of course not, of course not," said the teacher. "All right, well, Rupert, perhaps it's best if you collect your things."

Meanwhile, Rupert couldn't imagine what Aunt Hazelnut wanted with him. Perhaps Uncle Henry had sent her to fetch him for another time-travel adventure. It couldn't be that something terrible had happened to his family and they had for some reason sent Aunt Hazelnut for him, could it?

"Oh, Rupert, you didn't have a chance to finish your valentines," said the teacher, glancing at his desk and looking troubled.

"Don't be ridiculous, woman, we've more important things to worry about," said Aunt Hazelnut as she bustled Rupert into the cloakroom to grab the two extra shirts and holey sweatshirt that he hung on his hook when he got to class.

"And you'll miss the treats," said the teacher as Aunt Hazelnut continued to sweep him along, out of the cloakroom, through the classroom door, and into the hallway. Rupert turned back frantically to see if perhaps the teacher would come after them to hand him a cupcake or a cookie or even a Rice Krispies square, but she had already closed the door behind them.

"Well!" said Aunt Hazelnut. "You're well out of *THAT!*"

"What do you mean?" asked Rupert as they raced down the corridor and out the school's front door. "We've passed the principal's office!"

"Oh, we won't be bothering with *HIM*," said Aunt Hazelnut. "That was just for show. I never had any intention of talking to him. No, listen, Rupert, I wanted to take you on a little field trip. One I do every year. It's my favorite thing to do and I wanted to share it with you. Because, you know—and don't tell the others this ever, especially Uncle Henry—but I felt rather bad about that thing with the prizes at Christmas and I've been trying to think of a way to make it up to you. And what better day to do it, I said to myself, than Valentine's Day. The most dreaded day of the year."

"Didn't you like Valentine's Day when you were in school?" asked Rupert in shock, for he thought all adults suffered the happy illusion that it was a joyous day for everyone and had simply loved it when they were children.

They climbed into Aunt Hazelnut's car and began zooming along the snowy streets to downtown Steelville.

"LIKE it?" squawked Aunt Hazelnut. "I *LOATHED* it. All poor children loathe Valentine's Day. I was not a Rivers by birth, you know. I was a Macintosh. And all us Macintoshes were poor. We came up from Kentucky hoping to score big in the steelworks, but, of course, everyone just gave up. My people came from the hills and it often seemed to me that for us Macintoshes, giving up was what we did best. I went to the very same school you go to, Rupert. Joe Rivers was in my class. We were childhood sweethearts and our love never faltered. He married me right out of high school and we moved into the Rivers mansion with the rest of them, because that's what the Riverses do, live together like ants in an ant hill. That was fine. I wanted whatever Joe wanted. Then he died. He got a very bad case of the flu in our sixth year of marriage and that was that. And it was as if I were made of stone ever after. All my happiness died with Joe. The Riverses didn't kick me out, I will say that for them, but I had nothing there to remind me of Joe. The only things I had left of him, the only things that were truly mine, were the jewels he gave me each year on every conceivable occasion— Christmas, New Year's, birthdays (both mine *and* his), Valentine's Day (that made up for a lot I can tell you, I almost came to like Valentine's Day), our anniversary, Arbor Day . . ."

"Arbor Day?" said Rupert incredulously.

"Little brooches full of emeralds in the shape of trees. There wasn't an occasion or holiday he didn't shower me with jewels. Thousands and thousands of dollars' worth of jewels. Every year I think I will sell them and make my great escape from that house..."

"Don't you like it there?" asked Rupert in amazement.

"Would you?" asked Aunt Hazelnut, sneering.

"I think I would," said Rupert, thinking of Christmas dinner and all the fireplaces and soft beds. "If it were my home."

"But that's the thing," said Aunt Hazelnut, "it *isn't* my home, not really. Because you can marry all the Riverses you like, but if you're a Macintosh you will always be a Macintosh. The part of you that began life dirt poor will always be dirt poor. Your circumstances may change, but *you* don't change. I can never really fit in there, but I can't go back to my life with my family either. I'm not a Macintosh anymore, nor have I ever really become a Rivers. I thought I would become a Rivers if given the chance and there I *was* given the chance, but the fantasy of the person I would become—sleek and chic and with the perfect life and perfect hair and perfect clothes and perfect thoughts and feelings? Well, I never became that fantasy me. I was just me in another house. If anything, I was the same imperfect person but more bored. Every year I think I'll go to the Pacific Northwest and become a fisherman. I do like fish. If I sell my jewels then I can bankroll my mad escape that way. So every year at this time, when winter is at its worst, I go to the bank, to the safety deposit box where

I keep my jewels, and I visit them. I plan to take them out and take them to Cincinnati and sell them. I've got the jeweler all picked out and everything. But then... *it* happens."

"What?" asked Rupert, who was so enthralled with this account that he barely noticed them parking and walking into the bank.

"I look at them and instead of just jewels I see Joe's face staring at me and the look he gave me when he presented them to me. And I can't sell them. It is the only time I see Joe's face so clearly in my memory anymore—when I look at the jewels. I think that when they go they will take his face with them. So I put them back and return to the mansion and think, Maybe next year. But"—Aunt Hazelnut became suddenly brisk again as they strode across the bank's marble floors and to a door that said BANK MANAGER—"perhaps today things will be different. Perhaps I will find the courage to move forward. Perhaps you will bring me luck."

Aunt Hazelnut knocked sharply on the door of the manager's office.

"Mrs. Rivers!" said the bank manager, bowing and scraping. "How delightful. What can I do for you?"

"I'm here to visit my safety deposit box," said Aunt Hazelnut.

"Certainly," said the manager. "I'll just get my key. Have you yours?"

Aunt Hazelnut held up the key to her safety deposit box and the three of them went downstairs to a big vaulted room where both keys were used, and then the manager left Rupert and Aunt Hazelnut alone.

"Here goes nothing," said Aunt Hazelnut, pulling out the box and opening it. "Sit down in that chair, Rupert, with your legs held together."

Rupert did as ordered. Aunt Hazelnut opened her purse and took out a pillowcase which she spread neatly over his lap.

"Now," she said. "For the full effect."

And she dumped the contents of the safety deposit box onto his lap. It was, to Rupert, as if the heavens had opened up and dropped their starry skies upon him. He was certain nothing had ever glittered like this before. There were necklaces and earrings and bracelets and brooches, tiaras and rings simply dripping with rubies and emeralds and sapphires and diamonds.

"WOW!" said Rupert. "WOW!"

"Yes, as jewelry buying went, Joe was A-number-one," said Aunt Hazelnut.

They looked at the jewels in awe and silence for a moment, and then there was the sound of scuffling and shrieking coming from upstairs. Even in this vault they could hear it.

"Good heavens, what can be going on up there? Who goes around shouting in a bank? It has been my experience that a bank inspires the same hushed reverence as a church," said Aunt Hazelnut, opening the door and leaning out to hear better and then screaming as two masked men with guns pushed her back in.

"Stick 'em up!" they said.

KIDNAPPED

BEFORE THEY knew it, the masked men had scooped all of Aunt Hazelnut's jewels and even her pillowcase into a big bag, while Rupert sat trembling on the chair. Then she and Rupert were hustled upstairs. Everyone in the bank was lying face down on the bank floor. The masked men kept shooting their guns at the ceiling in a very noisy and chaotic way and this kept everyone from moving until the four of them had made it to the car and were roaring down the highway. The robber who sat in the front passenger seat kept a gun in each hand pointed at Rupert and Aunt Hazelnut, who sat in the back.

"This is a very dirty car," said Aunt Hazelnut conversationally. She kicked some empty Coke cans away from her expensive high heels.

"Yeah, sorry about that," said the masked man in the passenger seat. "We were going to clean it before we left but we didn't have time."

"I had to take my cat to the vet," said the man driving.

"Oh?" said Aunt Hazelnut. "Poor thing. What was wrong with it?"

"Fur ball."

"Now you see, that's why you don't want a cat," said Aunt Hazelnut, turning to Rupert. "You must get those brothers of yours to start stealing dogs. A dog is a proper pet. A dog will love you and stay at your side and be utterly dignified in his total *disregard* for his personal dignity in his pursuit of your happiness. A dog has his values in place. A cat is just another animal."

"I don't want my brothers stealing any animals," said Rupert, whose voice was quavering as he, unlike Aunt Hazelnut, found it impossible to forget he had a gun pointed at his head.

"No, you're right," said Aunt Hazelnut. "It's a scandal."

"They always put them back," said Rupert.

"Yes, but people say that's your mother's doing. If it were up to them, your brothers would keep the cats, that's what people say. Anyhow, my point is that everyone always talks about how cats are cleaner than dogs, but they aren't. Cats are always getting fur balls stuck in their throats, and when they're not doing that they're bringing dead mice into the house and spreading their entrails over everything. Is that what those demented cat people call clean?"

"I like my cat," protested the driver.

"Well, did you ever think how it's going to feel when you end up in *jail*?" asked Aunt Hazelnut. "Never mind. It won't care. Cats don't form attachments. Another reason to prefer dogs."

"The cat lives with my mother. Besides, we're not going to jail," said the man with the guns. "We just want your jewels and then we'll be off."

"Well, you can't have them. They're part of my escape plan," said Aunt Hazelnut, settling back into the seat and apparently relaxing. Whereas Rupert was fidgeting his hands like crazy and had the increasing desire to pee himself.

"Escape from what? What've you got to escape from, you're *rich*!" said the man with the guns.

"Not really," said Aunt Hazelnut. "These jewels are really all I own. The rest belongs to the Riverses and I live with them on sufferance. Have you ever lived anywhere on sufferance?"

"I guess not."

"You *guess not*," said Aunt Hazelnut, making a face. "Just as I thought. So don't speak of what you don't know. Besides, you probably wouldn't know where to sell them. You wouldn't get a good price. Now turn around and take us back." Aunt Hazelnut looked to Rupert. "Once again, I really don't think I can do it, Rupert. I thought this might be the year I'd go west and become a fisherman...But no, I saw Joe's face the instant I'd emptied the jewels into your lap and they lay there glittering. There he was on our first anniversary, handing me the diamond tennis bracelet. There he was on Washington's birthday, handing me the cherry tree necklace with its little ruby apples." Aunt Hazelnut wiped a tear from her eye.

"Good grief, Nutty, you *still* can't let go?" exploded the gunman. "It's been thirty years at least since Joe kicked it. What the heck's the matter with you?"

Aunt Hazelnut, who had taken a handkerchief out of her purse and was weeping quietly into it with bowed head, snapped her head back up at this. Then she peered very hard at the gunman as if trying to see through his mask. Her face hardened and her tone became brisk. "I should have known. I should have *known!* No one has called me Nutty since my salad days. It's Charlie Tanner and Chas Mackenzie, isn't it? Don't tell me it's not. The two of you have had nothing but stupid ideas as long as I've known you, but this has to be the stupidest. Didn't you think I would recognize you?"

"Aw, Nutty..." whined Charlie, lowering his guns as Chas drove on. "We didn't think we'd get someone we *knew.* We certainly didn't think we'd get *you.* Aw, jeez. The plan was to burst into the bank and scoop up whoever was in the safety deposit vault as a hostage along with whatever loot they had opened it for. We weren't going to actually hurt anyone. The guns were just for show. We were going to let the hostage go once we got away."

"How did you know someone would be in there?" asked Aunt Hazelnut. "You might have gotten down there and found the vault empty."

"We had an inside man, or rather woman. One of the tellers. Chas is dating her. Or was. I think probably this heist is gonna put a damper on that romance. We told her we were going to be in the café across the street and she should take a bathroom break and wave to us from the front window of the bank if anyone went down to the safety deposit vault."

"Well, I don't think much of that," said Aunt Hazelnut. "Do you think it's nice to get that girl in trouble like that, because someone is surely going to find out that she waved to you."

"Well, jeez, Nutty, we didn't tell her WHY we wanted her to do this and she didn't ask. She wasn't what you'd call the brightest lightbulb in the box. We figured, you know, she couldn't give us away if she didn't know why she did it."

"I didn't like her so much anyhow," said Chas.

"Well, that's just peachy, isn't it?" said Aunt Hazelnut. "You know, you boys were never geniuses, but you were never mean. You never pulled mean tricks like this."

"Well, you're one to talk," said Charlie. "Tell what's-his-face here what you did to *me*."

"Charlie and I dated," Aunt Hazelnut said primly to Rupert. "Briefly."

"But I thought you married your childhood sweetheart," said Rupert, beginning to relax too. This was turning into a much more casual kidnapping than he'd anticipated.

"Yes, well, but Joe took a little persuading after high school to actually pop the question. I had to threaten him with something. Men are so often like that, Rupert. It's women who want to nest, men just want to fly around and make bird noises. Anyhow, I threatened him with Charlie."

"It wasn't nice either," said Charlie.

"Oh, grow up and get a life," said Aunt Hazelnut. "That was all in the dim and distant past. And why haven't you turned the car around as I ordered you to, Mr. Chas Mackenzie?"

"Because we're not going back," said Chas. "Sorry, Nutty. Can't now. We'd end up in jail."

"I see," said Aunt Hazelnut, considering. "Then where are you taking us, if it wouldn't be too much trouble to tell me?"

"Our lair!" said Chas.

And they drove on.

Aunt Hazelnut and Rupert didn't speak after that.

Rupert returned to being frightened. He did not like the sound of a lair. It brought to mind the image of lions dragging their dinner to a big cave and storing it there. Aunt Hazelnut, meanwhile, sat sulkily leaning back in her seat, her arms crossed over her chest, and stared angrily out the window.

An hour later they reached the lair and drove into an old barn.

"What is this?" asked Aunt Hazelnut as they climbed out of the car.

"It's an old farm Charlie and I bought," said Chas. "We were renovating the barn."

"Turning it into townhouses," said Charlie. "You know, in the existing real estate market we figured we could triple our money."

"That's very nice," said Aunt Hazelnut. "But who would you find to live all the way out here? We're an hour out of Steelville and over an hour from Cincinnati. Unless you're raising chickens, I don't see the value in it."

"Yeah, well," said Charlie, scuffing his shoe in the dirt, "that's what we found out. And we kind of got in a bind moneywise."

"That's the problem with you boys," said Aunt Hazelnut. "That's *always* been the problem with you boys. You have an idea but you DON'T THINK IT THROUGH! Now, for instance, what are you going to do with Rupert and me? I mean, it's all very well to go around kidnapping people, but you can't keep them in mason jars. We're not preserves, you know. We're not jellies. Are you a jelly, Rupert?"

"No," said Rupert quietly.

"Exactly. Rupert is not a jelly. And I am not tomato relish. You should have just taken the jewels. Then you would have been plain old bank robbers. Now your charges will be compounded to kidnapping. And that's a very serious offense."

"Aw, you wouldn't press charges, would you, Nutty?" asked Charlie.

"Well, no, personally, I wouldn't," said Aunt Hazelnut. "And not for old time's sake either, but rather because I'm not that kind of vindictive person. Nevertheless, you've got the boy to think of. Now his people might press charges. Or more likely sue. In civil court for trauma, et cetera."

"He doesn't look traumatized to me," said Chas, studying Rupert.

"He looks a *little* traumatized," said Aunt Hazelnut. "That's not a happy expression he's wearing. Of course, he's the type who always looks a little traumatized. But that's not the point. The Browns are short of cash. They might see this as their ticket out."

"Ticket out!" scoffed Charlie. "You had a ticket out, didn't you, Nutty? Much good it did *you*."

"I never wanted a ticket out *per se*," said Aunt Hazelnut. "I only wanted Joe. And the right choice it was too. *He* wouldn't steal my jewels!"

"Oh, plunge a dagger through my heart, why don'tcha?" said Charlie, taking his mask off, tilting his head back, closing his eyes, and looking pained. "Aw, Nutty, did you really think I planned to keep your little all? I mean, I may have thought about it at first because of the way you dumped me, but in the end you should've known I could never do it. But we couldn't just leave you in the bank. We still needed hostages to get out. Here," he said, beginning to hand Aunt Hazelnut the bag of jewels when he suddenly startled and dropped it. The four of them were standing above a big hole in the barn floor and the jewels went right down a large pipe that was being put in for the plumbing.

"Oh JEEZ!" screamed Aunt Hazelnut, looking frantically down the pipe. "Look what you did, you butterfingers!"

But everyone else was too busy suddenly hearing what had made Charlie drop the jewels. Police sirens.

"You boys stay here," said Aunt Hazelnut, going out the barn door and around the corner of the barn to spy four police cars, lights flashing, sirens blaring, heading down the long farm driveway.

"Cheese it, it's the cops!" said Chas as Aunt Hazelnut scurried back into the barn.

"I told you, I *told* you this wasn't a good idea," said Aunt Hazelnut.

"Quick, get in the car!" yelled Charlie.

"Don't be silly, you can't win a high-speed car chase against four cop cars. Haven't you ever been to the movies? Stay in the barn. Rupert and I will go out and cover for you. Charlie, put your mask back on just in case. I'll tell them you never took off your masks and you abandoned us here and drove off with accomplices. That you got no loot, there was nothing but old love letters in my safety deposit box, but you wanted us as hostages in case you had a hard time getting out of the bank. And that I think you were heading for Cincinnati."

Rupert and Aunt Hazelnut left the barn, closing the door behind them. They walked around the corner to where the cop cars were almost upon them, and Aunt Hazelnut turned quickly to Rupert and said, "Listen, we'll tell the cops that you're friends with Turgid and I picked you up for tea and was going to just grab my love letters—I wanted to read them to you and Turgid on Valentine's Day or some such twaddle—and then we were going to surprise Turgid by picking him up. But we got kidnapped before we got a chance to go back to school to collect him."

"Why did you get me first?"

"Because you asked me to get you out of class early. You hate making valentines."

"Well, that's true," said Rupert. "What if the cops don't believe you and want to go into the barn?"

"Not believe me?" said Aunt Hazelnut, straightening her shoulders and lifting her head high and putting on her best socialite smile as the cops stopped their cars and got out. "Why wouldn't they believe me? I'm a RIVERS. Now come on, let's get a ride home."

But that was not that. The cops seemed to believe everything Aunt Hazelnut told them unquestioningly. Two cars took off for Cincinnati, one went back on patrol, and another gave Aunt Hazelnut and Rupert a ride to the police station, where they had to make statements about what had happened, and then the police gave them a ride back to Aunt Hazelnut's car, and finally Aunt Hazelnut dropped Rupert at home.

When Rupert walked into their living room his father was watching television.

"Just watched the news," said Rupert's father. He turned and stared at Rupert for a few minutes. Neither of them said anything. Rupert didn't know what was up. Finally his father barked, "Any word on how your kidnapping came out? HA!"

"Oh," said Rupert as light dawned. "It was on the news? I didn't see any cameras or reporters or anything."

"Well, someone got hold of the story. Did you think

you could keep it a secret? What were you doing with that Rivers broad anyhow?"

"She wanted to read us her love letters because it was Valentine's Day," said Rupert, floundering. "I think she was going to bring both me and Turgid for tea because I'm kind of friends with Turgid anyway although not really but Mrs. Rivers thought we were but she probably got me mixed up with someone else but then before we could get Turgid we got kidnapped so it was just me and Mrs. Rivers and then—"

Mr. Brown turned back to the TV, waving Rupert away. "All right, kid, I've already lost interest."

Rupert started upstairs when his father called, "You didn't have to actually listen to her reading her old love letters then?"

"No," said Rupert, stopping.

"Well, you dodged a bullet that time!" hooted Mr. Brown, and turned up the volume on the TV.

NEW LIVES

THE NEXT day at school Rupert was the center of attention. Everyone wanted to know what it had been like to be kidnapped, but Rupert didn't really want to talk about it.

"Oh, about average," he said when asked.

Finally, everyone let it go except Malcolm, the school bully.

"I asked what was it like," he said. "You want me to clobber your head?"

Rupert paused as if considering whether this would be a pleasant pastime in an otherwise dull day, and while he was thinking of an answer, Turgid charged up.

"Leave him alone," he said, stepping between Rupert and Malcolm.

"*Leave him alone,*" mimicked Malcolm in a singsong voice. "*Leave him alone.* Rich kid!" He spat provocatively on the ground in front of Turgid, but the bell rang and everyone had to go off to class.

"Thanks," said Rupert as they filed inside.

"No problem. I had to deliver a message from Aunt Hazelnut anyway. She wants to meet you after school on the corner of Elm Street and Maple."

"Okay, thanks," said Rupert.

All day he wondered what Aunt Hazelnut could possibly want with him. He had thought their adventure was over. He ran to Elm Street as soon as the final bell rang and there sat her car. Rupert jumped in and Aunt Hazelnut burned rubber pulling away from the curb.

"As you may have guessed, I am going back to get my jewels," said Aunt Hazelnut.

"I forgot all about them," admitted Rupert. "But won't the police be staking out the joint?" He had heard this expression once on television.

"Staking out the...? Why? I told them that the robbers didn't get away with anything and I wouldn't press charges. Of course, they're still wanted for creating havoc and firing off guns and such, but the police in Steelville are, to put it mildly, underachievers, so I think we have nothing to fear on that front."

They drove on a bit longer in silence. Then Rupert said, "But why am I coming?"

"You saw that pipe where the jewels fell?"

Rupert nodded.

"Well, I can't possibly fit in there, girlish figure

though I have. And neither can Charlie or Chas if they were stupid enough to stick around there. It takes someone about . . . your size . . ."

"Oh, right," said Rupert, who didn't like the sound of this at all.

"It's not like you have to go into a mucky hole," said Aunt Hazelnut with false cheer. "It's just a pipe."

"Right," Rupert said again.

"And afterward, to say thank you, I thought I'd take you someplace for a really good dinner."

"Oh, wow!" said Rupert, all thought of getting stuck or even perhaps *lost* in some horrible underground pipework vanishing at the thought of a whole meal.

"I'll take you to any restaurant you'd like."

"McDonald's," said Rupert unhesitatingly. He had drooled over McDonald's commercials for years. Everyone he knew, even the poor kids at school, seemed to have gone there. They got Happy Meals. The meals came with toys. He could eat the meal and bring the toy home to Elise. Or maybe he could even save her part of the meal. Although once he got started eating, as he knew from Christmas, best intentions though he might have, it was terribly hard if not impossible to stop. Maybe Aunt Hazelnut would buy Elise her own Happy Meal.

"McDonald's? I think we can do a bit better than *that*," said Aunt Hazelnut. "What about the Wilmar Steak House?"

"Oh no, McDonald's is really where I want to go. That's my choice," said Rupert. "Please. I've always wanted to go to there."

"Well, all right," said Aunt Hazelnut.

They drove in silence the rest of the way to the farm. When they got there they went into the barn and were surprised to find Charlie and Chas sitting on the fender of the getaway car.

"What kind of no-account police department doesn't even search the place?" asked Charlie. "Those cops didn't return once to see if we'd come back to the farm. I mean, I don't want to be arrested, but it's no fun being a master criminal when they make it so *easy* for you."

"Don't be ridiculous, you're no master criminal," said Aunt Hazelnut. "Not even close. I'd bet you anything the cops have been doing patrols to see if your car has returned to the farm. Better keep your car in the barn until you leave. And then better leave fast."

"Aw, do you always have to be so deflating?" said Charlie.

"How is Charlie ever going to have any self-esteem with you going at him like this?" said Chas.

"I only tell the truth," said Aunt Hazelnut primly. "It's one of the reasons Charlie loves me. Why aren't you boys long gone?"

"We thought we'd wait for you to return and help you retrieve the jewels," said Chas.

"Thank you," said Aunt Hazelnut. "That's very kind."

"And then, you know, I thought maybe you'd want to give us another chance," said Charlie, circling the dirt with the toe of his tennis shoe.

Aunt Hazelnut paused and stared into space for a moment as if framing what to say. Finally, she said, "That's very kind of you, Charlie. And a wonderful offer for someone. Only unfortunately not for me. My heart will always be with Joe. There's no accounting for these things. And the sooner you get over me and move on, the better."

"Yeah, well, I just thought I'd ask," said Charlie. "You know, 'cause I've got nothing else going on right now. I pretty well am over you anyhow."

"Really?" said Aunt Hazelnut, sounding not at all pleased. "Well!"

There was an awkward silence while everyone looked in different directions with varying degrees of irritation on their faces.

Finally, Chas said, "Well, let's get to it, shall we?"

"Yes, indeed, let's," said Aunt Hazelnut. "And let's shake a leg. *My* car isn't hidden in the barn. I want to be done and out of here in case the cops come looking. Now, I brought Rupert along to get the jewels out of the pipe. He's the only one of us who will fit, if I'm not mistaken."

"Good thinking," said Charlie. Despite his claims of being over Aunt Hazelnut, he seemed depressed. And in no hurry to get the jewels and race off. He sat on the fender chewing on the end of an old cigar and gazing through the open barn door into the distance.

"HURRY UP!" said Aunt Hazelnut. "Haven't you heard anything I've said?"

But when Charlie just looked at her glumly in response, Aunt Hazelnut sighed and walked over and sat next to him.

"Listen, you two geniuses got any other plans now that this bank robbery thing hasn't worked out?"

"Yeah, we got us some backup plans," said Charlie.

"Like what?"

"Well, in one you and I get married and live happily ever after," said Charlie.

"Right, we've already established that that's not going to happen," said Aunt Hazelnut.

"I don't see why not. It's not like staying true to Joe's memory will bring him back. I was lying before. I love you to pieces. I always will, Nutty."

"I know, Charlie."

"And I think you love me too."

"I suppose I do in a way. Or I could. I won't say there hasn't always been an exciting spark between us. If I hadn't met and married Joe, you and I might have been a thrilling match. But the thing is, Charlie, Joe just kind of wore me out. The way really big emotions sustained over time *can* wear you out. That part of me anyway. He loved me so strong, that sometimes, it was like he was wind and I was stone and it was eroding away what there was of me. I wasn't stone anymore. I was stone shaped by the wind."

"Didn't you love him too?" asked Rupert, for he was leaning against the side of Aunt Hazelnut's car listening avidly. This was another glimpse into the adult world of love and marriage, and totally different from the one Mrs. Rivers had given him. Were there so many different ways to be in a marriage, he wondered? How much was his parents' like either of these? Or was it something different altogether? It had always puzzled him. Why his parents weren't simply divorced like so many parents at his school.

"I loved him extravagantly. That's why I couldn't do it again. I couldn't be the receptacle of your love, Charlie, and I wouldn't want to. I guess I'll just take my jewels and go home. So tell me, what's your plan? You can't go back to Steelville."

"That's sure as shooting," said Chas.

"Well then, what?"

"We got a few ideas up our sleeves," said Charlie.

"Okay," said Aunt Hazelnut, nodding. "What's one?"

"We become astronauts," said Charlie.

Aunt Hazelnut gave a short bark of laughter.

"What? That's so funny to you?" asked Chas. "Like we got less of a chance to become astronauts than you have to be a fisherman or some such?"

"I'm sorry I laughed, boys," said Aunt Hazelnut. "But it doesn't seem like such a sound plan to me. I mean, I'm sure there're tests and things you have to take to be astronauts. They don't want two fifty-something-year-old boys from Ohio past their prime. You got to train up when you're young."

"You don't know that for sure," said Charlie. "I mean, what we may lack in youthfulness we can make up for in steady nerves and stamina. It's the old folks who have stamina, because they've been through so much they've had no choice but to endure. They know how to do it."

"Well, you might be right at that," said Aunt Hazelnut. "I sure shouldn't be raining on that parade." Then, as if she'd lost all interest in their career plans, she turned to Rupert. "Listen, Rupert, you gonna go down that pipe or what?"

"Oh, right," said Rupert, and walked over to the entrance to the big pipe. It had been installed vertically. He looked down its big black center but could see nothing at all.

"How am I supposed to go down this thing?" he asked. "I can't just drop down it. I can't see how far or where it goes. It's just a big dark hole."

"Well, I don't think it goes down too far, does it, boys?" asked Aunt Hazelnut to Charlie and Chas, who had come to peer down it with Rupert. "Not more than ten or twelve feet."

"Something like that," said Charlie. "Why don't you jump in and find out?"

"I don't want to jump into a big dark empty hole," said Rupert.

"Boy's got the sense he was born with," said Chas. "I got some rope in my car. Let's tie it around his waist and lower him down, Charlie."

So the rope was gotten and they lowered Rupert down the pipe. It wasn't too bad. It was dark but he could still see Charlie's and Chas's faces at the top and they didn't have to lower him too far. At the bottom he felt around on the ground and easily found the bag of jewels.

"GOT THEM!" he yelled up the pipe, and they pulled him back up.

"Well, okay then," said Aunt Hazelnut when Rupert had handed over the jewels. "I guess we'll be going and you boys are off to Florida to become astronauts. Is that where they train?"

"I dunno," said Charlie. "I guess we'll be looking into it. We could just head down that way."

"I think the place they train you for the circus is in Florida too," said Chas. "If we can't get into the program to become astronauts, we could maybe go to circus school."

"That sounds exciting," said Aunt Hazelnut. "Look out for the elephants."

"I don't like elephants," said Charlie.

"Who doesn't like elephants, what's the matter with you?" said Chas.

"I don't even like horses. If we're driving all the way down there, I think you should know that about me," said Charlie.

"Well, fair enough," said Chas, nodding.

"And you, you just heading back to put those jewels in the bank again?" Charlie asked Aunt Hazelnut. "That's it? Nothing new, no great ventures, no leaps forward for you?"

"NO!" shouted Rupert suddenly. He would not normally have had the courage for this, but somehow something seemed compelled from some deep part of him. Some part of him that had listened to this adult conversation, taken it in, and now couldn't help what he felt to be the truth of the matter from coming out. "Don't you see, Aunt Hazelnut? Joe didn't give you those jewels for you to visit them once a year and keep his memory alive. He gave them to you as a kind of security in case anything happened to him, so you had a way to leave and *find* your life. To finally find it after having been, well, part of something you weren't. Something you never were, twice over. Not a Macintosh, not a Rivers. He wanted you to find out who you really are. What good would he think it would do you to keep a bunch of jewels in a bank vault year after year? And he must have known you wouldn't wear them."

"No, I never have liked jewelry," said Aunt Hazelnut. "It itches me."

"Well, you see then. What you need to do is go sell the jewels; go sell them before you chicken out again. And head on out to the West Coast."

"To be a fisherman?" asked Aunt Hazelnut, imploring Rupert for information as if he were some sort of guru.

"Right," said Rupert a bit less certainly.

But Aunt Hazelnut took this response at face value and a wild look came into her eye. The hand holding the bag of jewels was trembling visibly. "I'm gonna do it. I'm gonna do it NOW!" she screeched, and ran to her car. "I'm gonna do it before I chicken out. Thank you, boys. I would never have done this without all of you. Thank you for everything!" She got in her car and zoomed off.

Rupert, Charlie, and Chas watched her car until it was a dot in the distance. Then Rupert said, "How am I supposed to get home?"

"Come on," said Charlie. "We'll give you a lift to the edge of town. Nutty is right, we gotta get out of here in case they got a patrol car going by periodically. And we don't dare head into Steelville in case Chas's teller girlfriend ratted us out. You don't mind walking from there, do you?"

Rupert shook his head. Visions of McDonald's danced through it. In all the fuss about new lives and trading in jewels, the dinner plan had been forgotten.

He wondered if he could ask Charlie and Chas if they were going to stop for dinner somewhere. Then he decided he couldn't. It would be too much like begging. It would be embarrassing.

Fortunately, the Browns' house *was* on the edge of town, so when Charlie and Chas stopped the car by the power station, Rupert only had a half block to go.

"I hope you haven't got too long a walk, kid," said Charlie.

"No, my house is right there," said Rupert, pointing.

"That's where you live?" asked Charlie.

Rupert nodded. Charlie and Chas looked at each other.

"Want to come to Florida?" asked Charlie.

"No, thank you," said Rupert, who wanted nothing so much at that moment as to eat his oatmeal and kitchen scraps and join his brothers under the bed. He opened his door and got out. "Are you really going to Florida?" he asked before closing the door.

"Yep," they replied.

"To be what—astronauts or circus performers?"

"I guess we'll have to see," said Charlie.

Rupert closed the car door and they drove off. He thought he would wonder all his life now if they had become one or the other. Or if Aunt Hazelnut ever became a fisherman. You only got bits and pieces of most people's lives, he thought. The only one you ever knew fully was your own.

But a couple of months later, when spring was just arriving, he got a bit more. He got a letter from Aunt Hazelnut.

Dear Rupert,

Although I don't want anyone to find me (so tell no one where I have gone, especially not the Rivers family), I thought you at least should know where your good advice has taken me. I cashed in my jewels. They were worth a bloody fortune, I must tell you. And I went to Seattle to be a fisherman. But I chickened out when I got to Pike's Place Fish Market. All those staring fish eyes. I didn't think frankly I was up to the job. Also, the boats I walked by on the docks smelled very fishy. It was off-putting. I didn't become this wild and free fishing person that I was in my fantasies. I was only me. It was disappointing to find that no matter where I took myself, I was still that, always only me.

So then I drove down the coast for a long way until I came to Mendocino. I stopped at a little B and

203

B and that night I fell asleep to the sound of the sea. And there I was a me I could be. Not a fantasy me. A happy me in a place that felt like this was where that me belonged. So I bought a little house. I am running it as a B and B. I have a tiny garden and a view to the sea. Every morning I get up and make scones. There is always another chapter in life, Rupert, and thanks to you I have found mine.

Your good friend,

Aunt Hazelnut

P.S. Burn this letter.

So Rupert did.

THE SUIT

EVERYTHING SETTLED down after that. When time went on, passing uneventfully, Rupert decided he'd had all the adventures with members of the Rivers family that he was apt to have. But things were looking up. Ohio was having a lovely, lush early spring. Tulips were blooming, the hillsides around Steelville were resplendently adorned in green grass. Big soft clouds drifted through the warm humid sky like illustrations from a children's book. His father, as he did every spring, stopped watching TV and instead moved his Trans Am out of the garage and into the driveway, where he spent all day tinkering on it. Rupert sometimes sat in the driveway to watch him. They never said anything to each other, but there was a companionable silence and it was pleasant to be able to sit in the sun again. Rupert had yet to take off one of his three shirts, but he was no longer cold all the time and, best of all, his feet weren't freezing and wet.

He was sitting contentedly in his classroom staring out the window as a persistent hummingbird tried to crash his way inside when the door of the classroom opened with a bang and there stood an officer of the law. He was a large, imposing man in a blue uniform and he had weapons attached to his belt. Everyone sat up a little straighter and Rupert's teacher startled.

"Can I help you?" she asked, a worried little frown puckering her forehead.

"Sorry to disturb," said the officer, "but I need to take Rupert Brown for the rest of the day."

"What did he do?" shouted one boy from the back, and everyone laughed.

"That's enough, children," said Rupert's teacher. "Rupert, gather your things. May I ask, Officer, what this is in reference to?"

"Mr. Brown here," said the officer (all the children were mightily impressed with Rupert being called Mr. Brown), "was a witness to a serious crime. We need him in for questioning."

"The attempted robbery and kidnapping again?" asked Rupert's teacher.

"But I've already done that," said Rupert in a small voice. He did not want to have to go to the police station again. He was also a little worried that the police had found either Aunt Hazelnut or Charlie and Chas and that he would somehow be in trouble for not telling the truth about it the first time. A police officer had also stopped by the school to question him and Turgid together in the principal's office after Aunt Hazelnut had disappeared. Rupert had said he didn't know where she had gone and had not heard from her. "After all," he had added in what he considered to be a clever touch, "it's not as if she and I were *friends*."

"No, of course not," the police officer had agreed. "But then why did she take you out of class?"

Rupert had looked stymied by this, but Turgid had jumped in and said that Aunt Hazelnut must have thought he and Rudy were better friends than they were because Rudy had been there for Christmas. The fact that Turgid kept calling Rupert by the wrong name even after the policeman had corrected him twice helped. And the officer left satisfied.

Or so Rupert had thought, but here was another police officer. He grabbed his sweatshirt and extra two shirts, threw them on, and traipsed down the hall, out the front door, and into the police car. He was allowed to ride up front but he was not comforted by the shotgun he had to sit next to. He did not think people should be driving around with shotguns in their front seats. Even the police. It was larger, heavier, and more dangerous-looking up close than he would have even imagined.

The officer said nothing except to inform Rupert

that his name was Officer Kramer and they would be explaining everything to him when they got to the interrogation room at the station. This sounded very scary to Rupert too.

Then when they were almost there Officer Kramer looked over at him and said, "You're kind of a skinny dude, aren't you?"

Skinny was hardly the word for it because Rupert had barely had a full or satisfying meal since Christmas. His cheekbones were beginning to stick out. He nodded.

"Don't they have a breakfast program at school?" Officer Kramer asked, parking the police car.

Rupert nodded again. How could he explain that no one liked the cat-stealing Browns and so he never got the free breakfast.

"Well, I'd avail myself of it if I were you. I've got two teenage boys myself and they eat like lions. Do you eat like a lion?"

Rupert shook his head. This was really an embarrassing discussion. He wished the officer would just take him inside and get on with it.

Officer Kramer shook his head and then led Rupert into the station and to a room with a table where a female officer sat.

"Officer Tomlin will be questioning you," he said as Rupert sat down.

"Hello, Rupert," said Officer Tomlin, smiling at him.

Then Officer Kramer left. Officer Tomlin asked Rupert how he was and hadn't the kidnapping been terribly scary and generally made small talk before saying, "Well, shall we get started?"

Officer Kramer returned just then and said, "Snacks," putting a container of chocolate milk and a bag of chips in front of Rupert.

"Excellent idea," said Officer Tomlin. "I always like snack time myself."

Now Rupert didn't know what to do. It sounded as if Officer Tomlin was planning on eating the chips and chocolate milk, but they were sitting in front of Rupert. He tried not to notice they were there. Officers Tomlin and Kramer meanwhile sat looking at him expectantly. Finally, Officer Tomlin said gently, "You can open your snacks and have them while we talk, Rupert."

Rupert demolished the lot in ten seconds. Officer Tomlin and Officer Kramer looked at each other over Rupert's head and then Officer Kramer said, "I think I'll just go get some lunch for Rupert from the café across the street. If we can bring it in for the jailbirds we can bring it in for the witnesses." And he left, muttering, "God's nightgown, what's the matter with this town."

"There now," said Officer Tomlin. "You mustn't mind Officer Kramer. He just likes to see . . . well—" She stopped, looked at Rupert's bashful face, and decided to change the subject. "Let's just continue while he's gone. I don't know how much Officer Kramer explained, but I'm not part of the Steelville force. I'm from Cincinnati. We've had a robbery and kidnapping in Cincinnati that's looking very similar to the attempted robbery you were a victim of. We would like therefore to question you and Mrs. Hazelnut Rivers again about what you can remember from that day."

"But I already said," protested Rupert, wondering wildly if Charlie and Chas were back and robbing safety deposit boxes in Cincinnati. Had they not been able to find lives as astronauts or circus performers?

"Yes, we know. You did a good job then too, Rupert. I've read the interview. But this is standard operating procedure, questioning the witnesses again. Sometimes we have to hear accounts of these things over and over because sometimes people remember more details in the retelling. Now you don't mind cooperating with us this way, do you? I know it must be very tedious and a little scary."

Rupert was shaking his head when the door opened. He thought hopefully it might be Officer Kramer with his lunch, but instead it was Uncle Moffat. Rupert was so surprised he said, "Uncle Moffat!"

"Are you related?" asked Officer Tomlin.

"No, not as such, not as such," said Uncle Moffat jovially. "But Uncle is what Rupert has heard me called. As he called Hazelnut Aunt, I gather. You see, Rupert turns up at the oddest times, at Christmas dinner, for instance, or in the bank vault with Hazelnut."

"But that was her idea. She invited me!" protested Rupert, who still couldn't get over the feeling that as a Brown he might be arrested for just about anything while held captive in this room.

"Right," said Officer Tomlin. She wrote something down. "As you and she herself said before. She wanted to read you her love letters. And now she's disappeared. And no one knows where she is."

"We've had a postcard from her from the world's biggest ball of string," said Uncle Moffat. "Says she was on her way to have her own life. Well, that's that, I say."

"I assume it was explained why you were brought in?" said Officer Tomlin to Uncle Moffat.

"Only one at home when you called, that's about the gist of it, isn't it?" said Uncle Moffat. "You want someone in the family to tell you where Aunt Hazelnut went, but as I said, we've no idea whatsoever. She was never a Rivers, you know, she just married my brother. She was a Macintosh by birth."

"Yes, well, we were hoping to question her too," said Officer Tomlin. "The timing of her leaving is interesting. And the fact that none of you expected it."

"Oh, now there you have it wrong," said Uncle Moffat, sitting down without being asked and sprawling comfortably as if used to owning whatever room he walked into. "We weren't informed in advance, but it isn't as if we didn't expect it. Truth be told, we had been expecting it ever since Joe died thirty years before. I mean, why stay? It wasn't her house. She hadn't been raised there. We always thought she must surely want her own life with her own kind, but no, she just stayed on. When she did finally leave we none of us were surprised, we were just surprised it took her so long. She might have given us an address where we could forward her mail, but oh well, you can't expect common consideration from a Macintosh."

"So you don't think it had anything to do with the attempted robbery and kidnapping, her disappearance?" asked Officer Tomlin.

"Why would it?" said Uncle Moffat. Just at that moment Officer Kramer returned with a burger and fries and started to reach across Uncle Moffat to put them down in front of Rupert when Uncle Moffat grabbed them in midair. "Ah, lunch brought in, I see. Very considerate of you." He scarfed them down before anyone could protest.

Officer Kramer cast a disbelieving look at Uncle Moffat and mumbled something about going out to get more when another policeman poked his head in the door and said, "Officer Kramer. You're needed. Robbery in convenience store on Third." And off he shot.

"Well!" said Officer Tomlin. "Rupert, we'll see

what we can do for you lunchwise later. Now, let me just get your statement. Let's see." She shuffled through her pile of papers. "Here it is. Rupert Brown, age ten, birth date...oh..." She stopped reading and looked up. "Birth date April 16. Today. I guess you're no longer ten, you're eleven. Happy birthday."

"Thank you," said Rupert, blushing.

"Well, we'll try not to keep you too long. Having a family party?" asked Officer Tomlin, smiling at him.

"Yes," lied Rupert. Rupert's mother always bought each child for his or her birthday a bag of menthol eucalyptus chips. These tasted terribly of cough medicine and nobody but Mrs. Brown liked them. To a family living on kitchen scraps they represented an extreme outlay of money, but even though they were a novelty and technically food, the children still could not stomach them and eventually they made their way back to Mrs. Brown, who always pretended to be surprised.

"Right then, let's just go through what happened one more time. And Mr. Rivers, if you could just listen to Rupert's story and see if any of it jogs your memory in regards to the account Mrs. Rivers gave you all when she got home that night. Perhaps you will remember something she told you that she forgot to tell us."

"Hmmmm," said Uncle Moffat, putting his hand to his forehead and thinking hard.

For the next hour Uncle Moffat and Rupert told and

retold, told and retold what they could remember. But nothing new came to light. Rupert was very proud of himself. He did not once let it slip what had really happened, and Officer Tomlin seemed to believe him.

"Well, thank you then, the two of you are free to go," said Officer Tomlin. "Have a good birthday, Rupert. Shall I have someone give you a lift home?"

"I'll do it," said Uncle Moffat.

"Right," said Officer Tomlin, and they were done.

Uncle Moffat and Rupert walked out to the car.

"Well, Rupert," said Uncle Moffat, "I guess we fooled them. The perfect crime!"

At first Rupert looked up in terror, thinking Uncle Moffat knew more than Rupert had thought, but then he realized that Uncle Moffat was just making a joke, so he laughed cooperatively.

They got into Uncle Moffat's huge Cadillac and Uncle Moffat said, "School's not even out yet. Look at that, you're getting a whole extra hour off from school and on your birthday too. Well, Rupert, what shall we do with it?"

"With what?" asked Rupert.

"Your extra hour," said Uncle Moffat.

"I dunno!" said Rupert. He couldn't figure out why they would be doing anything at all.

"I know," said Uncle Moffat. "Let's go downtown and buy you a suit."

"A suit?" Rupert repeated, sure he had heard wrong.

"Yes, every young man should be measured for a suit on his birthday. Do you own a suit, Rupert?"

"No," said Rupert.

"There, you see, every young man should own a suit, period. Now I've got a lovely little tailor on Fourth. Great fabrics. Give him a lot of business. He likes to keep me happy. If I say make up this suit right now, he'll do it on the spot. I'll show you how to choose a suit fabric and what to ask for in tailoring. It will be part of your education."

"All right," said Rupert. He didn't know how to say that he would never have any place to wear a suit. He would wear it to school for the warmth if he didn't know that the first time he did, he would be beaten to within an inch of his life. There was a whole crowd of toughs just itching to beat up anyone who did anything different and he knew better than to give them an excuse. Perhaps he could sleep in it though. He had heard of pajamas. Then he realized there was no way he could adequately explain the suit to his brothers either.

Uncle Moffat drove downtown humming all the way. The idea of the suit seemed to be making *him* very happy.

When they entered the tailor shop, Rupert saw that the walls were lined with bolts and bolts of fabric. How did anyone ever choose?

"My young friend here needs a suit, Bernie," said Uncle Moffat.

"I should think," said Bernie, sniffing. "Look at his shirt. There are *holes* in it."

"Now, now, Bernie, don't be a snob."

"When do you need the suit?" asked Bernie.

"Today," said Uncle Moffat offhandedly.

"TODAY?" shouted Bernie.

"Yes, within the hour. And we'll take seven shirts at the same time."

"*Ay yi yi*," said Bernie. "Well, you'll have to buy ready-made shirts then."

"I'll tell you what, we'll take one ready-made to walk out with today and you can make six later and call me when they're ready. There's no point having a suit specially tailored for the lad if he's going to wear some ill-fitting shirt."

Bernie made a face.

"Come, let's not be sullen about it. It's Rupert's birthday present. We're not walking out of here without a suit."

Bernie rolled his eyes. He called his assistants away from their sewing machines in the back of the shop and put a CLOSED sign on the door.

"Now, Rupert, let me show you what you want and don't want in a shirt," said Uncle Moffat.

He led Rupert over to a wall where ready-made shirts

were stacked up and down in piles according to color. There seemed to be thousands, millions of shirts lining the wall. Reds fading to oranges fading to yellows. Rows of dark blue fading lighter and lighter. Next to a row of greens doing the same. It was so beautiful. It was the most beautiful thing Rupert had ever seen. He felt a stab as he thought how his mother had told his father at Coney Island that one day she would have a suit and real crocodile pumps. How she would enjoy this. She had probably never been in such a shop, never seen how a suit was made. Why were the things that were supposed to happen to her happening to him instead? It seemed so unfair, but then he forgot all this as he was swept into having to make decisions. How did one ever pick a color or even seven with so many choices?

Uncle Moffat pulled a brown shirt off the wall. "This one is perfect."

"Oh," said Rupert, looking disappointedly at the muddy-hued fabric. "Couldn't we have at least one splendid color?"

"Don't be ridiculous," said Uncle Moffat. "I was a boy in this town. I know about mud. And chocolate. I bet you're fond of chocolate, aren't you, Rupert?"

"Yes," whispered Rupert wistfully.

"Now let's look at the suit fabrics."

Uncle Moffat had Rupert feel all the fabrics. There were worsted and cashmere, cotton and linen, polyester, velvet, and silk. There were different weights to the fabric, from seven ounces to fourteen.

Finally, after much deliberation, Uncle Moffat said, "Well, Rupert? I've tried to educate you as best I can. Now it is time for you to make a decision."

"I'd like the warmest, heaviest suit possible," said Rupert. "Fourteen-ounce wool, please. In a tight, warm weave."

"Right, we'll take silk," said Uncle Moffat. "The boy doesn't know what is what. It's spring. Summer is coming. Don't worry, Rupert. It's only your first time choosing a suit. You obviously took in none of my instruction, but that is why I am here to guide you. Now, let's see, let's have it in plain brown. Nothing too fancy."

"Silk it is," said Bernie, whipping the bolt Uncle Moffat had chosen out of his hands. He took Rupert's measurements and then whisked the fabric away to be cut and sewn and made into a suit.

Next Uncle Moffat educated Rupert as to shirt fabrics. Rupert chose a nice cotton poly blend that didn't require ironing.

"Right, linen. Summer coming again," said Uncle Moffat. "Would you like to choose the colors?"

Rupert started to nod when Uncle Moffat said, "Of course, you wouldn't. You have terrible taste." And quickly picked out a brown linen that he thought would work well for the remaining six shirts.

Half an hour later a brand-new brown silk suit and a ready-made brown shirt were on Rupert, and his old clothes were in a bag. Bernie had begged Rupert to let him burn his old clothes, but Rupert, of course, had not agreed to this.

"Now, don't you look a treat, if I do say so myself," said Uncle Moffat. "You see, Rupert, money can buy happiness. Just look at yourself."

Rupert was standing in front of the three-way mirror and had no choice but to look at himself, but he had to admit that he looked wonderful. He looked like a different person. He looked, despite his age, like a person of means and culture. A cut above his fellow man. He looked, he thought—*important*. He looked more important than Uncle Moffat because, as he discovered, it wasn't just owning a good suit that made a person so but how they wore it. Uncle Moffat was portly. There was no other word for it. His cheeks were red as if his blood pressure was too high. He looked always on the verge of a good sweat. He looked, if truth be known, so bloated it was as if he were about to pop. Rupert looked cool and calm and collected. He was so thin he was like a human clothes hanger, and this, it turned out, was just what it took to show expensive clothes to their best advantage.

"You ever done any modeling?" asked Bernie, putting the last stitch in the hem of Rupert's pants. "You oughta consider it. You got the build. You got interesting bones in your face too. Wouldn't have noticed it the way you were dressed before."

"Yes, Rupert," said Uncle Moffat, nodding agreeably. "I'd be proud to take you anywhere *now*. In fact, yes, I *will* take you somewhere. Somewhere special. Now where shall that be? I'll take you to my club for a late lunch. Haven't had lunch yet and I'm starving. Are you starving, Rupert?"

Rupert wondered what Uncle Moffat considered the hamburger and fries that he had eaten at the police station, but he certainly wasn't going to argue against a meal and so nodded his head vigorously instead.

"Ah, yes, of course, you are. Probably always hungry. Boys *are* always hungry. I was always hungry as a boy. Then the Union Club is the place to go. We can show off your new suit. We can have a good, proper lunch the way only the club can make it. Like hamburgers, Rupert? The club makes them the size of your head. They make French fries the size of your fingers. They make milk shakes the size of Niagara Falls. Let's go."

Rupert was so excited he could almost not contain himself. He was *finally* going to get a decent meal. Normally he would be terrified to go to some rich person's club. He couldn't even imagine what such a place would be like except that it would be itching to throw out someone who looked like him. But with the suit on he had a sudden new confidence. He felt he could strut in anywhere and be treated like someone special. As if he had finally done the special thing he had always suspected that he would.

Even walking to where Uncle Moffat's car was parked, Rupert had the heady new sensation of people looking at him and not, for once, in a disapproving way. People coming toward him and Uncle Moffat on the sidewalk automatically made way for them as if they were royalty. How Rupert wished he could wear his suit all the time.

At the Union Club, a man in a uniform fairly ran up to open his door and take the car from Uncle Moffat. He drove it away to park it. Imagine, thought Rupert, if you're rich, someone parks your car *for* you. Then Rupert and Uncle Moffat got into an elevator and rode up and up and up. The Union Club restaurant was on top of the tallest building in Steelville. If you could afford to dine there you knew you were on top of the world.

At the entrance to the club the maître d' greeted Uncle Moffat by practically bowing from the waist. "Your usual table, sir?"

"Yes, James," said Uncle Moffat.

"May I take your bag, sir?" the maître d' asked Rupert.

Rupert clutched his bag closer. What did the maître

d' want with his bag? Would he get it back? Uncle Moffat saw Rupert's frightened expression and said, "No, thank you, James. He likes to keep it close. Now, bring us menus immediately. It's this young man's birthday and we're celebrating."

"Yes, sir, right away," said the maître d', and showed them to a table at a window looking down across Steelville's river. But you could see beyond that to the steelworks and even beyond that to what looked like the edge of Ohio itself.

"Like the view, Rupert?" asked Uncle Moffat.

"I never knew you could see so far!" said Rupert, his nose upon the window glass. "It's *splendid*!"

Uncle Moffat laughed. With his new suit on, Rupert even *talked* differently.

"Yes, it is, yes, it is, Rupert. My whole life is splendid. I am a splendid man. Now pick up your menu and decide what to have."

Rupert already knew what he wanted. He wanted a hamburger. At school Friday was hamburger day and orders were put in to McDonald's. Any child could bring money from home and one would be delivered at lunch. Rupert had never had a hamburger but he had drooled watching other children eat theirs. He had made a vow that if he ever had money he would eat a hamburger. He had gotten close when Aunt Hazelnut had promised to take him to McDonald's, and very close in the police station when Officer Kramer had brought him a lunch he almost got to eat, and finally now it was his chance. He ordered a hamburger and fries and the largest milkshake on the menu, which was called the lalapalooza and guaranteed to give you a bellyache, which Rupert simply could not wait to feel.

After they had ordered, Rupert looked around the room, and that's when he found that the people eating at the Union Club were stealing shy looks at him and nudging each other as if to say, *What a remarkable looking young man, what a good-looking child. And what a suit!*

"Do you ever bring Turgid or the other Turgid or Sippy or Rollin or any of the other cousins here?" he asked suddenly.

"Oh yes, we've all eaten here, but the children don't like it. They find it stuffy. The other Turgid once crayoned on the tablecloth and had to be spoken to. In general, it isn't the best venue for children, but you are behaving wonderfully, Rupert. You haven't once kicked a waiter. Kudos to you."

Rupert contemplated what it must be like to have the kind of life where you didn't like eating someplace like this because they wouldn't let you crayon on the tablecloth or kick the waiters. When he was done looking at the people who were all dressed in fancy suits of their own, he looked at what they were eating. And *my,* what people had for lunch. And for such late lunches. Why it was after three o'clock and they were only now plowing into steaks and giant salads, whole lobsters and huge desserts covered in whipped cream. Rupert's mouth began to water. He had drool running down his chin and had to keep mopping it up with his napkin, which he had put on his lap right away to copy Uncle Moffat.

Uncle Moffat was moving restlessly from side to side in his chair and drumming his fingers on the table.

"The service here is usually better than this. They seem to be taking their time today. I *am* so sorry, Rupert," he began, when suddenly a bevy waiters appeared through the kitchen door. They had two huge trays, and on them were Rupert and Uncle Moffat's hamburgers. Rupert's was covered in sparklers that spelled out Happy Birthday Rupert. They were the biggest, sparkliest plates of food that Rupert had ever seen, and as the waiters made their way to them in a long, slow line like monks in procession, they began to sing a chorus of "Happy Birthday." At that, everyone in the Union Club joined in. They not only joined in, they stood up. There was a whole restaurant full of impeccably dressed rich people solemnly singing to Rupert. Nothing so extraordinary had ever happened to him. He was quite sure nothing so extraordinary would ever happen again.

"Ah, a little club tradition," said Uncle Moffat. "The singing of the rich. Well, enjoy it, Rupert, boy."

Rupert did enjoy it but part of him was thinking, *Just Bring Me The Food!* As the wonderful greasy smell of grilled meat and potatoes wafted toward him it was all he could do not to run the few steps over to the waiters and grab his food right off the trays. When at last the waiters began to put the trays down on an empty table preparatory to setting the plates before Uncle Moffat and Rupert, there came a whirring sound and the ground began to shake.

"TORNADO!" cried Uncle Moffat, emptying the breadbasket and putting it on his head like a helmut.

"Earthquake!" said a waiter crawling under a table.

And then suddenly between the waiters and Rupert's table appeared a large cardboard box, and standing in it were Uncle Henry and Turgid.

"What the heck," said Turgid. "I thought you said this was a time machine. Why, all it's done is take us to the boring old Union Club."

THE PRESIDENT

THE WAITERS froze. Everyone in the restaurant froze except the maître d', who came scurrying across the floor with his hands outstretched.

"Mr. Rivers, sir," he addressed Uncle Henry. "How good to see you again. Master Turgid. Let me take that carton for you—"

"NO!" shouted Turgid. "Don't touch the time machine."

"Turgid!" said Uncle Henry reprimandingly.

"Sorry," said Turgid. "Didn't mean to be rude. But we don't know how much time we have. This thing just swooped in here and may swoop out at any second."

"Have you been *inventing* again?" barked Uncle Moffat reprovingly. "I thought you promised to stop all that."

"Rupert?" said Uncle Henry, his eyes suddenly falling on him. "Is that Rupert? Wearing a *suit*?"

"Yes," said Uncle Moffat, shifting uncomfortably on his chair. "And what of it?"

"Well, he looks ridiculous is what of it," said Uncle Henry.

Rupert blushed. Up until that moment he had imagined himself quite dapper and the envy of every eye.

"He doesn't," said Uncle Moffat staunchly. "He looks smart. Doesn't he look smart, James?"

"Quite smart, sir. And if I may say so," said the maitre d', glancing nervously at Uncle Henry, for both he and Uncle Moffat were important patrons, "somewhat ridiculous too. In the best possible way."

"Oh, for God's sake, James, quit prevaricating," said Uncle Henry, and then turned to Uncle Moffat. "Did *you* buy him that suit?"

"Uncle Henry," interrupted Turgid, "can we just *go*?"

"*Why* did you buy him a suit?" asked Uncle Henry, ignoring Turgid altogether.

"If you must know, it's his birthday."

"Oh," said Uncle Henry. "Happy birthday, Rupert. Yes, but why a *suit*? I'm quite certain from the little time I have spent with him that a suit is the least welcome of presents. As it would be for any normal boy."

Am I a normal boy now, wondered Rupert? He had mixed feelings about this. To be normal meant that he was like the other boys regardless of his poor-edge-of-town-Brown status. That was good. But it also meant he was no longer special. He found this quite troubling and deflating.

"Yes, happy birthday, old fellow," said Turgid, who also, as soon as he arrived in the Union Club, began to talk differently. "Many returns of the day."

"Well, then, having lunch at the club are you?" said Uncle Henry. "To celebrate? Splendid. Shall we join you? What are we eating here?" He reached over to the table where one of the trays rested and stole a French fry. "My, the club makes good fries."

"As if we have all the time in the world," said Turgid, rolling his eyes. "Come on, Rupert, get into the time machine with us. We'll take you someplace better than *this* to celebrate."

"You will not. I am not done atoning," said Uncle Moffat.

"AHA!" said Uncle Henry. "You're not taking him here because it's his birthday. You're taking him because you feel bad about the prizes. And that's strictly, *strictly* against the rules."

Rupert felt like saying to Uncle Henry, *Well, it's no more than* you *did*, but he kept quiet.

"You know as well as I," Uncle Henry went on, "that you are not allowed to feel bad about someone losing and you are not allowed to make up for it. Come on, Rupert, because he broke the rules, Moffat will have to forfeit your company."

"I shall not. Stay right where you are, Rupert," said Uncle Moffat. "And let's have lunch."

"Yes, let's have lunch," whispered Rupert, looking at the food longingly, but no one heard him.

"Oh no you don't," said Uncle Henry, scrambling out of the box.

He went right over to Rupert, who barely had time to snatch his bag of clothes before Uncle Henry lifted him out of his chair and heaved him into the box. For a skinny guy he had remarkable strength. Then, just as he prepared to hurdle back into the box himself, it started its characteristic whirring noise and the next thing Uncle Henry knew, he was standing next to nothing but food-laden tables staring at the space where the time machine had been.

"Well, I'll be dipped in batter and deep-fried," he said in amazement.

"Yes," said Uncle Moffat. "Now see what you've done? Rupert has had to forfeit his birthday lunch. That's very unsporting of you."

"Nonsense, I'm sure Turgid will find him something to eat wherever they turn up. And when will you learn that children don't like the Union Club anyway?" asked Uncle Henry.

"Poppycock, Rupert was having an excellent time until *you* showed up," said Uncle Moffat.

"Hmmm, this does look delicious though." Uncle Henry grabbed Rupert's plate decorated with the sparklers which had now burnt down to nothing. He pulled them out, pulled up a chair on the other side of Uncle Moffat, put the plate in front of himself, and commenced eating without further ceremony. "Waste not, want not," he said through a mouthful of burger.

Everyone in the restaurant had remained standing throughout this whole event and now that the show seemed to be over sat down and resumed their own meals. They weren't terribly interested in how the appearing and disappearing box trick had been performed. They were rich and used to being splendidly entertained. Now they had important eating to do and then must get back to their other important tasks of the day.

Uncle Moffat sighed, signaled the waiters that he was ready to be served as well, and, when his plate was put in front of him, dug into his own food.

"I do wonder where they have gone," said Uncle Henry, his shoulders hunched over his mammoth burger and his mouth full of lettuce and tomato. "Somewhere where the food is good, I hope."

Turgid and Rupert wondered the same, for it was seconds later that the time machine deposited them in the middle of a large room with a big desk in it.

"Aw," said Turgid. "This just looks like someone's house."

Rupert looked around. It didn't look like someone's house to him. The room was large and grand and yet somehow it felt institutional. He could not put his finger on this except that it was as if someone very stodgy had done the decorating. It was a little too perfect. He suddenly understood what his mother meant when she laughed and said their house didn't lack the lived-in look, for that was exactly what this room *did* lack. And yet it looked familiar, as if he had seen it somewhere before—in photographs, perhaps. There was a big round rug in the middle of the floor with an eagle on it. There was an enormous desk and a couple of large windows and some couches.

"Turgid," he began excitedly as it came to him, when the door to the room opened.

A woman came in saying, "Mr. President," and then she stopped and screamed.

Turgid and Rupert jumped. Rupert looked down worriedly to make sure they had not damaged the bottom of the box.

"How did you get in here? Oh my God, Mr. President," began the woman again, clearing her throat and trying to get a hold of herself. "What has happened to you? Who has *done* this to you?" And she ran from the room.

"I think we're in the Oval Office of the White House," finished Rupert in a whisper.

"Of course," said Turgid, who had seen pictures of this room as well. "But where is the president? I don't see anyone."

"Perhaps she thought he was in the box with us," said Rupert. "Perhaps she thought we were bundling him away in it."

This didn't sound very likely, but they had no more time for speculation. At that moment a number of men and women in blue suits with earpieces came racing in.

"You see!" said the woman running in behind them. "It's just like the pictures of him as a boy. It *is* him as a boy. Someone has de-aged him from sixty-nine to a child!" She quickly found a photo on a shelf and held it up next to Turgid for the others to see.

"Yes, well, perhaps a nephew," said one of the men. "That seems more likely than your idea that the president has suddenly aged in reverse due to some evil plan perpetrated by this one." He pointed to Rupert.

"No, no plan," rattled Rupert nervously. "Not evil."

"The president has no nephews. None at all," said the woman. "As his personal assistant, I know everything about the president, and if he had a nephew I would know about it. You ought to know too, you're the Secret Service, after all."

"Well, maybe a distant cousin," said the Secret Service agent patiently.

"For heaven's sake, just ask him," said another agent. He turned to Turgid. "How do you know the president, young man?"

"I don't," said Turgid honestly. "I came here via

magical box." This sounded more reasonable to him than *time machine*. *Time machine,* he decided, had been so overdone as to be unbelievable. But you didn't hear a lot about people getting around via magical box.

"You see," said one agent turning to another. "It's just some kids visiting the president and playing around. Where's the president gone, young man? And who is your well-dressed friend?" For Rupert, of course, was still wearing his fine silk suit.

Turgid and Rupert looked at each other, the same thought going through both their minds. It was one thing to let a room full of Ohio business people lunching at the Union Club see them appearing in magical boxes. It was another to appear before top security people in the nation's capital in such a conveyance.

"Oh, the president? No idea. Haven't seen him in yonks," said Turgid airily. He had heard this expression on a BBC television show and thought it struck just the right note of upper-class laissez-faire.

"Don't get smart with me, young man," said one of the agents, and then realized that these boys might be friends of the president or the children of top diplomats and he changed his tack. "Say, would you like to come along with me, boys, and have some milk and cookies in the kitchen while we sort this out?"

"Oh, yes, please," said Rupert.

"No, thank you," said Turgid, throwing Rupert a look.

But two of the agents came over to them anyway and lifted them bodily out of the box.

"There now, how shall we dispose of this box?" they asked.

"And what have you done with our president?" wailed the personal assistant.

"And what's in the bag?" another asked Rupert.

"My old clothes," said Rupert, clutching it tightly. If they took away his old clothes he'd be sunk when he finally got home.

"For heaven's sake, Helen," said one of the agents, turning to the personal assistant, "you should know where the president is."

Rupert breathed a sigh of relief when no one questioned him as to why he was carrying old clothes in a bag.

"He can't have left here without you seeing him," agreed another agent.

"But he didn't, I swear; he never left the room."

"We've done nothing with him, honestly," said Rupert.

"Well, we might have roughed him up a little," said Turgid, who when he got very nervous, tended to become punchy. He giggled. "And can we have our box back please? It's rather special."

The man holding it looked uncertain. "I think we need to go over this with lasers and X-ray and chemical detectors first. Might be anything. Might be a weapon."

But an agent who had a more kindly eye said, "Oh, for heaven's sake, Andrew, don't you remember what it was like to be a boy? Didn't you ever play in a box? Give them the carton. Let's get them a snack and sort things out and figure out where the president has gotten to."

Rupert and Turgid were led down a series of long corridors in a parade of three security men and the president's personal assistant, who was now in possession of the box and carried it away from her body as if it might have cooties.

But halfway down a dark hallway one of the men stopped and said, "Why don't we just do a quick DNA swipe of the two to be certain before we head to the kitchen?"

"Good idea," said the others.

Rupert and Turgid quickly found themselves at the public entrance to the White House, where visitors were put through a metal detector, X-rayed, and then DNA-swiped before heading onward.

The boys had the inside of their cheeks swabbed by a bored-looking security guard.

"Now, we just wait a few minutes for a computer match and then we can go get your cookies," said a secret service agent while the security guard punched in numbers and waited.

A moment later something popped up on the screen that made him frown.

"This isn't possible," he said. "It simply isn't possible."

"What isn't?" asked one of the agents. "Isn't there a match?"

"Well, this boy's match says he is one Rupert Brown, American citizen. But this boy..."

He read the results again as if he couldn't quite believe it. "This boy is Turgid Rivers."

"That's right," affirmed Turgid.

"Oh," said an agent. "So he's related to the president, after all?"

"No, according to his DNA, he *is* the president," said the security guard.

"I told you so," said the personal assistant, clutching the box.

There was a moment of silence, and then instead of being whisked away to the kitchen the boys were whisked away to some other room in the basement of the White House. Calls were made and then a whole other group of people converged.

"All right, boys," said a very important-looking man. "I hear that one of you has the same DNA as the president of the United States, and what I want to know is: who are you and how did you steal the president's DNA?"

"I didn't steal anything!" protested Turgid.

"Are you a clone?" said the very important man, banging his fist down on the table.

"Impossible," said a woman in a lab coat. "Can't be done. If this boy has the president's DNA, then this boy is the president."

At this all the people in the room turned to Turgid and studied him as if he were a petri dish that had grown something incomprehensible.

"We can't have the United States being governed by a ten-year-old."

"I'm twelve," said Turgid. *"He"*—he pointed to Rupert—"just turned eleven today."

"Yes, that's very nice, Mr. President, but the question we have is are you the clone or the original in altered state? Do you remember vetoing the anti-Zadeski garbage bill this morning?"

"Not really," admitted Turgid.

"I don't believe you're the president in any form," said another agent.

"Please, this *must* be the president you're talking to," said the personal assistant. "Sir, can I get you one of your Nutella doughnuts? That always makes you feel better."

"Yes, please," said Rupert.

"No, thank you," said Turgid, throwing Rupert a look. "Listen, there has to be a mistake. I can't be the president. It just wouldn't happen. I have never wanted to be president."

"The other possibility," said a woman who had just entered, having been called down to the meeting room to help as soon as the DNA results showed up, "is that someone has found a way to turn back time for the president's DNA so that he is getting younger and will no doubt soon shrink to embryo size. What I like to call the Dorian Gray effect."

"He doesn't seem to have gotten any younger since we got here, Doctor," said an agent. "He *looks* the same."

"Now, listen, here's the thing troubling me," said another agent. "I accept that the leader of the free world has somehow been youthened to the age of twelve. But the question I have is who is this sidekick, this Rupert Brown, and what was he doing in a box with our president?"

"I'm just me," said Rupert stupidly. He couldn't think how else to explain it. He was starving and wished they'd just bring on the Nutella doughnuts and stop all the speculation.

"Enough. Give me the box," said the doctor. "I will take it away to be tested immediately."

She snapped her fingers and the personal assistant clutched it all the tighter saying, "This box belongs to the leader of the free world!"

"That's right!" shouted Turgid.

"All right, Mr. President, perhaps you would like to *explain* the box," said the very important man.

"Um, um, um," stalled Turgid. "I'll tell you what, I will be happy to explain it, but we have to *show* you how it works. Rupert, will you get into the box with me, please?"

Everyone looked at the very important man and he nodded his permission.

The personal assistant put the box down and two Secret Service agents headed to Turgid and Rupert to lift them into the box. Once inside, the boys waited hopefully for the familiar whirring and whizzing and for the box to carry them to any time but this one, but nothing happened. Rupert's heart did a nosedive. If the time machine stopped working, they were stuck here, in some future time in Washington, D.C. What would become of them?

"I see," said the very important man. "I see that this box does nothing. Men, take it away."

"WAIT!" shouted Turgid. "We have to be in the sunshine. I promise you that I will show you how the box works once we are outside. You must believe me. After all, you voted for me."

"*I* didn't," said one of the agents, and everyone turned to glare at him.

"We can't be shut up in a room and feel comfortable and, uh, talkative," Turgid continued, "and, uh, able to do effective demonstrations."

"Take them outside," said the very important man. "After all, what can they do in the sunshine they can't do here? They can't get away with all of us surrounding them."

"Besides," said the personal assistant, "I've never known the president to want to get away. His life has been devoted to duty. His values are family, country—"

"For pity's sake, Helen, the election is over," said the very important man rudely.

Two of the agents picked up the box with Rupert and Turgid in it, and they all trooped down the hall again to the entrance of the White House and then down the front steps, which the security men had cleared for them. The agents put the box down and stepped back respectfully.

Rupert couldn't imagine why Turgid was so insistent upon going outside. Even if they could get out of the carton, surrounded as they were, they would never make it off the lawn of the White House.

But Turgid clearly did have a plan, for he whispered in Rupert's ear, "At the count of three, say *Up!*"

"*What?*" whispered Rupert back, sure he had heard wrong.

"Say *Up*. I've no time to explain. One, two, three . . ."

And so Rupert dutifully said *Up*. He said it with all his heart and soul. He said it with no idea what it meant. And to his surprise, without the usual whirring noises, the carton simply rose. It rose straight up so quickly that before he knew it, the faces of the upturned Secret Service agents and all the White House staff were just dots on the ground.

"Now," said Turgid, happily turning to Rupert. "It's *your* birthday. Where would you like to go?"

HIDING

SIDEWAYS!" SAID Turgid before Rupert could answer and before they shot up into space. The box stopped its ascent and began traveling at a more leisurely pace, across the D.C. sky. It was slower than a helicopter but faster than a hot air balloon and just as eerily quiet.

"WOW!" said Rupert, looking down over the side of the box, for the boys were getting their first glimpse of the cars of the future. Even without the wonder of these, all of Washington, with its great buildings and monuments, was laid out below. Then Rupert got dizzy and had to sit down.

"Uncle Henry told me that he'd discovered by accident that the box can travel this way as well as through space and time," said Turgid, leaning casually over the side of box, not bothered at all by the height. "Look at those people going on some kind of thing you stand on and it moves along hovering *over* the sidewalk. They're not walking! They're not on anything wheeled. What's making them go? Wow."

Rupert stood up to see this and then sat down again.

"That's the Lincoln Memorial and that's the National Mall, kind of a big park, and that's the Wall, the Vietnam Veterans Memorial," Turgid continued excitedly, pointing down.

"How do you know all this?" asked Rupert.

"My dad took me and Sippy and Rollin here last year. He had business and he let us come. We saw almost everything, but what I really wanted to see was the National Air and Space Museum. I wanted to see the *Spirit of St. Louis*, Lindbergh's plane. We never did though. We ended up having to leave before we could get to that museum because we took too long at the National Museum of American History. We couldn't drag Sippy away from Judy Garland's ruby red slippers from *The Wizard of Oz*."

"So then let's go see the *Spirit of St. Louis* now," said Rupert.

"Really?" said Turgid. "It's your birthday. You should be the one to pick."

"No, I don't even know what's here, so I have no picks. Besides, if it weren't for you, for your whole family, I would never have had any of these adventures," said Rupert expansively, and then he immediately regretted it. Suppose Turgid asked what other adventures? He didn't want to give away any family secrets.

But Turgid just nodded, looking rather troubled for reasons Rupert couldn't guess, and said, "Down."

"Is something bothering you?" Rupert asked.

"I'm just trying to figure something out," said Turgid, and then they landed in a tree.

This was convenient more than not, for the leafy branches hid the boys as they folded up the box as best they could so they could carry it with them without attracting attention. The boys then slid down the trunk and landed with a plop. This drew some looks, for in Washington, D.C., people were not used to seeing boys sliding out of trees, especially one in a silk suit. But the boys walked on looking as though everything was quite ordinary, and after that no one paid them any mind.

Turgid had five dollars with him, so they went into a convenience store, bought a couple of Cokes, and asked for the largest bag they had. Because Rupert was wearing a silk suit, they got it. Then they sat outside on a bench, drank the Cokes, and put the box in the bag. Because Rupert still carried his bag of clothes, Turgid took charge of the bag with the box.

"Where is the National Air and Space Museum?" asked Rupert when they had finished their Cokes. The Coke was so wonderful it merely whetted his appetite for more. He wanted to ask Turgid if they didn't have money for something else. A candy bar perhaps. But, of course, he could not.

"I'm not sure," said Turgid, "but I remember it's on the Mall, so if we just walk around the Mall we'll see it. I'm sure we've time to look at the *Spirit of St. Louis* before those agents figure out where we landed. After all, they don't know where we were headed, and even if they somehow saw the box go down from that distance with some futuristic device we can't imagine, it will take them some time to catch up to and find us."

As it turned out, the boys spotted the National Air and Space Museum within minutes of walking the perimeter of the Mall and dashed over. But as they reached it, Rupert stopped. "How do we get in?" he asked. "We only have the change from your five-dollar bill."

"It's free," said Turgid. "All these national museums are free."

Rupert was suddenly filled with pride to be a citizen of a country that opened its national treasures to everyone free of charge.

"To think," he said as they walked up the museum steps, "that someday you'll be president of this great country. I've been wondering about your DNA and—"

"Yes, me too," interrupted Turgid. "And I've tried to find any other explanation, but I can't. The only way I can have the president's DNA is if we time traveled to the future to a time when I *am* president. It's the worst news I've ever had in my life. This is terrible, Rupert, and I don't know how to fix it."

"Why do you need to fix it? It's a great honor! And now you know what you'll be when you grow up, and that it's not just something good—it's something SPECIAL."

"That's just the problem!" wailed Turgid suddenly. Several people turned and looked at them. "That's just the problem," he whispered this time. "I don't want to be president. And now I know I have to be. All the other things that I think I might want to be, all the other possibilities, are gone. My life now totally lacks imagination. But as bad as that is, now with the time machine not working, I'm worried I'll be stuck here and have to lead the free world as I am. And I'm not ready. My teacher says I am very advanced for twelve, but I'm not advanced enough for that."

Rupert thought back to traveling with Uncle Henry and how they had speculated that only one version of yourself could exist at any one time. Now he thought this might be the case, for it sounded as if the president had disappeared when the younger Turgid showed up in the Oval Office. But he couldn't tell Turgid this without revealing his adventure with Uncle Henry and he wasn't sure Uncle Henry would want him to do this. Also, he thought, what difference did any of it make?

The thing was to see the *Spirit of St. Louis* and get back to their own time.

"So let's try to get out of here. Let's take the time machine someplace private and get into it again," said Rupert. "Maybe it was just a blip, like when you're on a computer at school and the Internet doesn't work for a minute and then it does."

"Maybe," said Turgid, but he still looked troubled.

The boys stopped speaking at that moment, all thoughts of time machines driven from their heads, for as they chatted they had entered the museum and before them hung the *Spirit of St. Louis.*

"He went across the ocean in *that?*" said Turgid breathlessly.

"Wow," said Rupert. "Wow."

"And *that's* another thing I now can't be," said Turgid. "A pilot. I don't want some stupid old desk job governing the United States. I want to fly!"

"Well, maybe you'll become a pilot *and* the president."

"Shall we ask someone? Do you think the average citizen would know if his president was also a pilot?"

"I think first we should find a bathroom and try the time machine before those secret service agents who are probably hot on our trail find us. Who knows what they will do to us after seeing our box fly away like that? Maybe this time they will throw us in some prison and we'll never get out."

"Good point," said Turgid, and the boys fled to the nearest men's room. There they went into the largest stall, opened the box up, and, with a great deal of difficult maneuvering, got into it. They stood hopefully while the minutes ticked by, but the box didn't whir or vibrate.

"This box is dead," said Turgid mournfully. "At least in terms of time travel. Oh, now what? Mother will have kittens if I'm not home by supper. And Uncle Henry will never be able to explain it. Mother is a very practical person. She'd never believe stories of a time machine."

Rupert thought he knew a few things about Turgid's mother that Turgid didn't, but of course he couldn't give away Mrs. Rivers's secret.

"The time machine can't be dead," Turgid said desperately. "It can't be. We must be able to find a way to fix it."

"Well, I've had a sort of idea," said Rupert shyly, for ever since Turgid had mentioned the ruby red slippers something had been stirring in his brain.

"What?" asked Turgid. "Hurry. I feel sure we're going to be found and captured any second and it's making me very nervous."

"I don't know . . . it seems sort of stupid," said Rupert.

"For heaven's sake. Anything is better than nothing, and I have no ideas," said Turgid.

"Well, suppose we take the time machine to the

National Museum of American History and put it next to the ruby red slippers. Maybe some of the magic from the slippers will seep into the time machine."

"You're right," said Turgid. "That is stupid."

Rupert's face fell.

"In the first place," said Turgid, "the ruby red slippers were a movie prop. They weren't *real* magic."

"Well, on the other hand, some people might say this is just a box," said Rupert, rallying.

"True," said Turgid.

"And you said that something is better than nothing."

"True," said Turgid.

"And I hear the sound of people running around," said Rupert. "They could be looking for *us*."

"Fold up the box, quick!" said Turgid. "And let's get out of here."

The boys left the stall, folded the box and put it back in the bag, opened the men's room door a crack, and peered out. They could see two men in dark suits with earpieces striding briskly about the entrance of the museum.

"They could be the museum's own security," said Rupert.

"They're pacing back and forth like something important has happened. Like they've just been told to be on the lookout for two boys and a box," said Turgid.

"We need a disguise," said Rupert.

As he said that, a school group began departing one of the museum exhibits and heading toward them for a bathroom break before leaving.

"We'll mix in with them," said Turgid. "They're roughly our age. We'll try to get into the center of the group and go out *that* way."

Rupert and Turgid had an agonizing wait while the boys in the group used the men's bathroom, washed their hands, threw wads of paper towels into the waste-basket as if they were playing basketball, and, as far as Rupert and Turgid were concerned, generally *wasted time*! But finally the group gathered together again and Rupert and Turgid made sure they muscled their way in among the boys exiting the bathroom. Then, because the school group was raucous and chattering and the teacher was more than a little done with them, Rupert and Turgid managed to get out of the museum surrounded by the clustering children without any-one paying attention to them. Once outside, they broke away from the group and walked quickly to the National Museum of American History.

"What if they have guards on the lookout for us there too?" asked Rupert as they approached it.

"We need another school group," said Turgid, looking frantically around, but unfortunately there was none readily available. What they did spy was a nice-looking older couple about to go in.

"Excuse me," said Turgid, going boldly up to them. "Do you think we could go inside with you? We'd feel better going in with an adult."

"My goodness," said the woman. "The two of you are awfully young to be out on your own, aren't you? Where are your parents?"

"Oh, they said we could meet them inside," said Turgid. "We've never been here before and we wanted to stand outside and soak up the atmosphere."

"Well, that sounds rather odd, dear," said the woman, clearly smelling a rat.

"No, I understand," said the man, who was the type to take pride in being the one in any group who *did* understand. "But, boys, there's all kinds of lowlifes here in Washington, same as everywhere. I bet you're from a small town, aren't you? Probably someplace people don't even lock their doors at night."

"We're from Steelville, Ohio," said Rupert.

"There, you see?" said the man. "Listen, you tell your parents not to let you roam about like this. You never know what strange characters you might come across. Now, you come in with us and we're going to keep an eye on you until we deliver you to your parents."

"Oh, that won't be necessary," said Turgid.

"I'm sure once we get inside we'll be fine," said Rupert.

"But maybe you could hold our hands until we get in," said Turgid, looking up with what he hoped was a lost-puppy look.

"Hold your hands?" said the woman.

"Come on, Matilda, the poor boys are terrified, I can see it in their eyes," said the man. "They've probably never been outside Ohio."

"No, Rupert hasn't," said Turgid.

"There, you see?" said the man again, grabbing one of Turgid's hands. Rupert grabbed hold of Matilda's hand with the one of his that wasn't clutching his clothes bag. She looked none too pleased about it but could hardly tear her own away without appearing surly. "Now come along, we'll all find your parents together."

It was lucky for the boys that Turgid had had the idea of holding hands with grown-ups, for inside were two pacing security guards, obviously alerted to look for the boys. Their keen eyes scanned the room over and over and stopped for a moment on the foursome before moving on. They were not looking for two boys with their grandparents.

"Now, where did you say your parents would be?" asked the man.

"By the ruby red slippers," said Turgid.

"All right. Matilda, why don't you get us a map," said the man, "and we'll head there straightaway."

Matilda tried to let go of Rupert's hand but he clung to her like a barnacle. Together they went to the information desk for a map. Then the four of them made their way to the ruby red slippers. There was a small crowd around the display. As soon as they managed to move next to it, Turgid whipped the time machine out of the bag and the boys jumped into it.

"Hey," said the man. "What are you doing?"

"I knew there was something fishy about all this," said Matilda. "I bet this is an advertising stunt."

"Which two of you people are the parents of these boys?" the man asked the crowd, ignoring, as usual, Matilda's input. People looked at the four of them and then drifted away pretending not to have noticed the boys in the box, the way people do when strangers start behaving in peculiar ways.

Rupert and Turgid stood in the box and held their breath, but there was no sign of life from the time machine.

"Oh, please, please, please," muttered Rupert. And then something even worse happened, for they heard the sound of running footsteps, and a host of Secret Service agents with earpieces, including the very important man, came dashing into the hall.

"THERE THEY ARE!" one of them yelled. "I told you the kid was wearing a *suit*!"

"We should have had you change!" whispered Turgid. "We forgot about the suit. Idiots!"

"Are those your parents?" asked the man confusedly.

"Of course they aren't. They're security men," said Matilda. "Oh, Morris, why do you always think you know what's going on?"

"I don't understand, where are the boys' parents?" asked the man.

"Oh, what are we going to *do*?" said Turgid frantically. "How are we to get home?" He clung to Rupert's arm in fear, when Rupert suddenly had an idea.

Home. That was the magic word in the movie.

"There's no place like home, there's no place like home," Rupert began, clicking his heels as best he could, squashed next to Turgid in the box. "You do it too!" he ordered Turgid.

"Maybe they're filming a movie scene," said Matilda.

"Don't be ridiculous, where are the cameras?" asked her husband.

"There's no place like home, there's no place like home," Rupert and Turgid said together, and suddenly there it was, the faintest whir, like a cat's subsonic purr.

"Get them!" shouted the agents, but just as they reached the box, the vibrations rattled Turgid and Rupert to their core, and the next thing they knew there was a whoosh and they had arrived somewhere new.

Turgid, peeking out of the box, said, "This doesn't look like Kansas to me, Toto. And it doesn't look like home either."

"Oh no," whispered Rupert, and pointed to the edge of the box. There they saw the ten white-knuckled fingers of someone clinging to the outside of it.

It was an agent who had just managed to grab the box as it took off. He looked at the boys in terror.

"Great," said Turgid. "*Now* what are we going to do?"

A FRIEND

THE AGENT let go of the box and lay on the floor staring at the ceiling. It was all too much for him to take in and he kept whispering, "This cannot be happening."

"Shh, no one invited you," said Turgid rudely. "We're sorry you tagged along, but it's your own fault."

"Although you were just doing your duty," put in Rupert. "Where do you think we've landed?"

"It looks like someone's kitchen," said Turgid.

Rupert and Turgid climbed out of the box and went with the agent into the next room, which was a large screened-in porch, and what they found there astounded them.

"Aunt Hazelnut!" said Turgid.

Aunt Hazelnut, who had been sitting delicately at her tea table sipping tea, stood up and screamed. Whatever the boys had been expecting, it was not this.

"Don't worry," said Turgid, swiftly running over to her, grabbing her arm, and quelling an urge to put his hand over her mouth. "We're not ghosts or hallucinations or anything."

"Yes, we're very real," said Rupert, hanging back. Despite their adventures together, he didn't feel he knew her well enough to grab her appendages.

"Oh lord, I should have known! You found me, you found me!" Aunt Hazelnut continued frantically. She raced outside to the front of the house and then back in again. "Where are the rest of them?" she asked breathlessly.

"The rest of whom?" asked Turgid.

"The family. The Riverses. You've tracked me down. You've tracked the Rivers to her source! HAHA-HAHA!" Aunt Hazelnut sounded completely hysterical. Her laughter chilled Rupert to the marrow. Who would have thought that a woman who had been so nonchalant about a little kidnapping would completely lose it at the prospect of visiting relatives? "And who is this man? Your private eye?"

"It's just us," said Turgid. "And a Secret Service agent from our nation's capital."

"Oh, sure it is. Sure it is. That's what they told you to tell me, isn't it? When they dropped you off? Tell good old Aunt Hazelnut he's a Secret Service agent and then she'll never expect it when he throws his butterfly net over her."

"Why a butterfly net?" asked Turgid with interest.

"NEVER MIND THE BUTTERFLY NET!" yelled Aunt Hazelnut, marching into the kitchen to see if there were any more Riverses lying in wait there. "Wait a second, that box in the corner. That's what you're going to entice me into, and then you'll send me back Federal Express or, if you're being really cheap, Parcel Post."

"For God's sake, Aunt Hazelnut, get a grip!" said Turgid as they followed her back to the porch.

But she turned to Rupert instead and pointed a long, skinny finger. "YOU! I never thought YOU would betray me."

"I didn't! I haven't!" protested Rupert. "We didn't even ask to come here. That box you saw is our time machine. It brought us by magical means."

"Oh, sure, magical means. Time machines." Aunt Hazelnut eyed them suspiciously. "And how ever did you come to be dressed like that, Rupert? And what are you clutching so in that plastic bag?"

"Uncle Moffat bought him a suit," said Turgid. "He has his old clothes in the bag."

"I guess that makes about as much sense as the rest of your story," said Aunt Hazelnut sourly, sitting at her tea table again.

Meanwhile the boys were looking around. They had expected to find themselves back in the Riverses' attic when the time machine stopped whirring. After all, when Dorothy famously chanted there's no place like home, the ruby slippers *took* her home. At the very least, the boys expected to find themselves in Steelville. Turgid looked out the window as waves broke far beyond the shoreline and out to sea and exclaimed, "Where *are* we?"

"Mendocino," said Rupert without thinking. He, of course, knew where Aunt Hazelnut now lived. It was supposed to be a secret, but he supposed that since they were standing directly in front of Aunt Hazelnut, the secret was out.

"Where's Mendocino anyway?" asked Turgid, looking around.

The screened-in porch had a stunningly beautiful view more apt to be appreciated by those who hadn't been whizzing around from the future to the present and across the country in such a short time. But even so, Rupert caught his breath. He had never seen nature so magnificent. And he had thought *Cincinnati* was a sight! His respect for Aunt Hazelnut increased sevenfold. He himself, if escaping Steelville, might have gone no farther than Cincinnati and its delights, but Aunt Hazelnut had kept driving and found this paradise on earth.

"Rupert, close your mouth, you're drooling on the linoleum. You're in California, Turgid," answered Aunt Hazelnut, who was beginning to recover herself. She decided that even if they were hallucinations, they could at least be tidy ones.

"How come *you* knew where we were?" Turgid asked Rupert.

"Because I told Rupert," said Aunt Hazelnut. "I wrote to him and I entrusted him with my secret."

"Why?" asked Turgid. "Why did you tell him and not us?"

"Because I had a right to do so as a person on the planet Earth," explained Aunt Hazelnut snippily.

"Oh, right, whatever then," said Turgid in hurt tones. He sat in a chair in the corner of the room and looked out at the gardens as if there wasn't much point in going on. He was glum. "Nobody tells me anything *and* I have no future."

As often happens when things don't go one's way, Turgid had decided to heap up a pile of grievances and suffer them all at once.

"What's wrong with *him*?" Aunt Hazelnut asked Rupert.

"He just found out he has to be the president of the United States when he grows up," said Rupert. "He finds it very depressing."

"Stuff and nonsense," said Aunt Hazelnut. "All little boys and girls want to grow up to be president of the United States."

"Not him," said Rupert.

"Well, buck up," said Aunt Hazelnut. "I'm sure they serve pudding at the White House. You like pudding,

Turgid. You can probably get pudding round the clock if you're president."

Meanwhile the agent had gotten up, dusted himself off, and was sitting at Aunt Hazelnut's tea table with a strange expression. It was a mixture of bafflement and something else. It took Rupert a moment to analyze the something else and then he realized what it was. The Secret Service agent had google eyes for Aunt Hazelnut. This surprised Rupert, for Aunt Hazelnut was old—well into middle age, he thought. He supposed she was all-right-looking in a fiftyish way, but that was not how the Secret Service agent seemed to be looking at her. He was looking at her as if she were a movie star. Of course the agent looked to be roughly the same age as Aunt Hazelnut, so perhaps he didn't mind her oldness so much.

"John Reynolds," he said, stretching a hand across the table for Aunt Hazelnut to shake.

"Hazelnut Rivers," said Aunt Hazelnut. She looked into his eyes as she shook his hand and startled, as if surprised to find something there she had not expected to see. She dropped her eyes shyly after that.

"What are you doing in Mendocino?" asked Turgid, no longer wishing to discuss the presidency. It was just as he feared. Nobody really understood his burden. It was lonely at the incipient top.

"Reflecting on my life and running a very profitable

bed and breakfast," replied Aunt Hazelnut. "That is, I was reflecting on my life until *you* came along. Oh well, if my reflections must be interrupted, I may as well give you the tour. Some are born hospitable, some achieve hospitableness, and some have hospitality thrust upon them."

Aunt Hazelnut stood up briskly and walked out of the porch, through the kitchen, and into the main part of the house. The boys followed her in a daze. As did the security man. Rupert and Turgid didn't quite know what to do with him.

"This is my parlor. It's a small parlor, but then it's just a small bed and breakfast. I have this main cottage with two bedrooms upstairs, and two small cabins with their own bathrooms. I had to put those in, Rupert, which just about used up the rest of the jewel money."

"The *what*?" asked Turgid.

"Never mind," said Aunt Hazelnut. "You two didn't say how long you'd be staying. I have one free cabin as it turns out, but only until tomorrow night, when I have more guests arriving."

"Oh, we can't stay, I suspect the time machine will return us shortly," said Turgid.

"I'll take the cabin," said the agent.

"How can you?" said Turgid. "Won't anyone be looking for you back home? Besides, you belong in another time."

the truth, I had planned on *this* being my evening meal because I planned to eat quite a bit of it, but I don't mind sharing with you. Rupert, open that drawer there and get the candles and matches."

As she said all this Aunt Hazelnut opened a cupboard and took out a cake plate on which rested a magnificent pink birthday cake. Rupert startled. How did Aunt Hazelnut know it was his birthday? And how did she get a cake on such short notice that it was simply waiting for their return to the cottage? He opened the indicated drawer and took out a box of striped birthday candles and a book of matches. Then Aunt Hazelnut stuck the candles on top and carried the cake to the table. She went back for four plates, four glasses, four forks, and some birthday napkins.

"There. A party," she said when they were all sitting around the table.

"I don't understand," said Turgid, who obviously had the same questions Rupert had. "How could you know we were coming? *We* didn't know."

"Of course I didn't know," said Aunt Hazelnut. "Pure happenstance. But I was going to have the cake anyway. You young people are so self-absorbed. You think only *your* birthdays are important. Oh yes, some old lady surely wouldn't care if her birthday passed without balloons or cake. *She* has no feelings. Only the *young* are allowed to celebrate, I suppose? I mean, I *can* have a cake, can't I, Turgid? You *will* allow me that, I hope."

"You're hardly old," protested the agent. "I don't consider myself old at fifty-three and I'm far older than you."

"No, you're not," said Turgid. "You haven't been born yet."

"He must have been born," protested Rupert, and tried to do the math, but his head was spinning with all the tricky time figuring.

"I meant *old lady* as hyperbole, of course. Although fifty-three is hardly old either," said Aunt Hazelnut, casting a gracious, glittering smile on the agent. She clearly had no intention of divulging her exact age. "It *was* beginning to seem like a rather lonely birthday. I'm happy, of course, to have ended up here. It is an excellent place to commence this next chapter of my life. I should have really done it years ago and I feel like for the first time I'm stretching my limbs, as if I've been cramped in some stall like a horse that never leaves the barn. I want to race about and whinny. I didn't tell any of *you* where I was going, Turgid, because I didn't want you all descending on me with family visits or feeling you had to make any effort to reconnect or *crowding* me with your advice. People do so like to give you advice when you're alone."

"I know!" interrupted Turgid, suddenly excited.

"Rupert has a wretched life. You're all alone. You can adopt Rupert! That's why the time machine took us here!"

"NO!" shrieked Rupert and Aunt Hazelnut before they could stop themselves. Then they both recovered their composure and Aunt Hazelnut glared at Turgid.

"For heaven's sake, Turgid," she went on irritably, "that's exactly what I'm talking about. You can't help horning in with ideas about what I SHOULD do. People, despite what you think, want their own lives in all their imperfect glory, rather than some idealized version where there's no dimension. People want good things, bad things, as long as they're THEIR things. Now, I told Rupert about moving here, but, of course, it never occurred to me he'd show up with family members and time machines and whatnot. I mean, why would he? Anyhow, it's been a breath of fresh air, this place to myself. No one to tell me what to do or comment on my life. But the downside to that is, quite naturally, a bit of emptiness. It is hard not to feel a bit empty when you're alone. That everything's a little sterile. I enjoy watching the sun set into the ocean every night by myself. Or that's what I keep trying to tell myself, but it's a lie. I see the beauty of the sunset all right, but it turns out you can't just see, you have to be seen."

John Reynolds looked at her with admiration.

"Perhaps you're missing pudding," said Turgid.

"Don't get smart," said Aunt Hazelnut.

"But I still don't understand how you knew Rupert would be here on his *birthday*," said Turgid, who had no interest in Aunt Hazelnut's pensées or John Reynolds's google eyes.

Aunt Hazelnut started to speak when Rupert, who had suddenly understood, interrupted her. "No, don't you see, she was celebrating *her* birthday, she doesn't know it is mine too," he finished lamely in barely a whisper, for he suddenly realized he was announcing his own birthday.

"Oh, *that's* what Turgid was getting at when he wondered how I knew you were coming," said Aunt Hazelnut. "Well now, that *is* a coincidence, Rupert. Then we must blow out the candles twice and you must make a wish too."

She struck a match and lit the candles, politely insisting Rupert go first. Rupert closed his eyes and wondered what to wish for, and the image that came, the image that seemed to be hanging there always right behind his eyelids, was a big juicy hamburger. All to himself. And maybe two. *I wish for* hamburgers, he thought, and blew out the candles. Then Aunt Hazelnut relit the candles, closed her eyes, wished and blew them out again.

"What did you wish for?" she asked Rupert after she'd opened her eyes.

"I *would* like some cake," he whispered, hoping she would mistake this for his wish. Even he knew that you weren't supposed to tell anyone your wish or it wouldn't come true.

"What did *you* wish for?" John Reynolds asked Aunt Hazelnut, but at that moment a loud whirring sound began and the floor vibrated.

"EARTHQUAKE!" cried Aunt Hazelnut.

"Quickly, stand in a doorway, it's the strongest part of a building," said John Reynolds, who, of course, as a Secret Service agent, knew these sorts of things. Then he did something extraordinary. He ran around the table, picked Aunt Hazelnut up as if she weighed nothing at all, and carried her to a doorway.

Rupert, Turgid, and Aunt Hazelnut looked more stunned by this than the earthquake.

"No!" said Turgid. "Not earthquake! Look at the time machine! It's vibrating. It's going to leave without us if we don't hurry."

The boys ran for the box and scampered into it.

"Put Aunt Hazelnut down, Mr. Reynolds," said Turgid. "You can't stay here or you'll be stuck. You'll never get back to your own time."

"I think..." John Reynolds paused, making no move to join them. He was still holding Aunt Hazelnut even though they now knew they weren't having a quake.

"Yes, do…" said Aunt Hazelnut, looking into his eyes. But whether she was saying do stay or do get in the box, the boys would never know, for the box began shaking harder, and the next thing they knew they found themselves on the floor of the Riverses' attic.

"Now he really is stuck," said Turgid. "He should have jumped in when he could. Aunt Hazelnut has no time machine to help him back to his own time."

"It didn't look like he wanted to return to it," said Rupert. "Do you think Aunt Hazelnut wants him there or not?"

"Who cares?" asked Turgid. "He's silly to stay in this time. Now by the time I'm president he'll be dead."

This was a strange and sobering thought.

"Well, it's a crap time machine if you ask me," Turgid continued. "We said there's no place like home and it didn't even take us home, it took us to Mendocino."

"Yes, I've been thinking about that and maybe it was because the agent was hanging onto the box. Maybe it took him to what will be *his* home. Maybe even if things don't work out with Aunt Hazelnut, he's meant to be in Mendocino at this time for some reason. Or maybe it's nothing to do with him, maybe the time machine would have taken us there whether he clung to the box or not so that Aunt Hazelnut wouldn't have to spend her birthday alone."

"Or maybe it was so you got a piece of birthday cake before your birthday was over."

"But I didn't get any cake," protested Rupert.

Turgid began pacing the attic floor. "I just hope they don't blab to anyone about who is going to be president. What if she tells everyone she knows and someone tells the newspapers and it gets back to Steelville? I would die if anyone found out."

"Why would anyone believe them?" said Rupert. "And don't worry, I'll never tell."

"Probably not, but let's write it in blood," said Turgid, scouring the attic for a knife. He finally found one in an old tackle box. "Here. This will do. Stick out your finger."

"I don't want to cut myself with that thing," said Rupert. "It looks rusty. We'll get lockjaw."

"Not me. I've had a tetanus shot. Oh, all right," said Turgid, throwing the knife on the floor. He went hunting again in boxes and old dresser drawers until he came across a sewing kit. "Well, here's a needle then. Prick your thumb and I'll prick mine."

Turgid wrote in pen on a bit of scrap paper he found that neither of them would breathe a word about the presidency. Then they both made an X in blood by their names.

"There," said Turgid when they were finished. "Now you are my brother."

"Really?" said Rupert.

"Or at least a very good friend. If you ever need anything, anything at all, you can come to me. Ever since Christmas when you participated in the games, you've become like one of us. You're a family member practically."

"Wow," said Rupert. He was so touched he felt like crying. Partly, he suspected, this was because he hadn't eaten in so long.

They sat and looked at the momentous document they had just signed.

"Who will hang on to it?" asked Turgid.

"It had better be you," said Rupert. "I don't have a place to keep things private."

"All right," said Turgid.

"TURGID!" Mrs. Rivers called from downstairs. "Dinnertime!"

"That clever box got us home in time for dinner," said Turgid.

"I've got to change back into my clothes," said Rupert, who still held the bag of old clothes as if for dear life. Now he put them back on and put the suit and new shirt in the bag.

"Come on," said Turgid, and they went downstairs. He led Rupert to the front door.

"See ya," said Turgid.

"See ya tomorrow," said Rupert.

"Yeah, see ya at school," said Turgid.

Rupert walked home. Turgid had said they were friends! He had a friend! It was the best birthday present imaginable. It changed everything!

When he got home his mother was just coming in the door and heading to the kitchen to start the evening oatmeal and kitchen scraps. She looked at him as usual, as if she couldn't quite focus in her fatigue. He smiled anyway and ran upstairs. He would have liked to show her the suit, but he felt instinctively that she wouldn't want to see it. That it would only make her angry that he had it. Where to hide the suit? The only things he owned besides his clothes were the raggedy blanket and pillow kept under the bed. It was the only place he might put the suit and be sure none of his siblings would come across it. The pillow had no case, but he went downstairs and took a kitchen knife and made a slit in the pillow. Then he jammed the suit in there. The rest of the family were watching TV. He went downstairs to join them. His mother was passing out bowls of oatmeal. On Rupert's she had made a smiling face with raisins she had bought on the way home for the occasion.

"How come he got raisins?" asked one of Rupert's brothers.

"It's his birthday," said their mother gruffly. "So

273

leave him alone. And after dinner I've got a special treat for you, Rupert."

"What's he getting now?" asked another brother.

"A bag of menthol eucalyptus chips!" said his mother. "All for him!

SURPRISE

RUPERT AWOKE the next morning with a sense that something had changed. It was the feeling you have when it has been winter for months and you wake up to the spring sound of birdsong and notice the first budding of the bushes. Something new and better has come along. It took Rupert a few minutes to remember what this was and to realize it wasn't just a post-dream delusion. Something *had* changed. He would see Turgid at school today. He had a friend.

Rupert ate his thin oatmeal while daydreaming about what this might involve. Perhaps they would sit next to each other in the lunchroom. Maybe Turgid would even share his sandwich, which Rupert decided wasn't really charity. Not when it was your *friend*. Of course, Rupert had nothing to share in turn, but perhaps you didn't keep count with friends. Or perhaps Rupert would come up with equally valuable things for

Turgid. Maybe he would come up with the idea that would help Turgid circumvent the presidency.

Rupert hurried out the door. He wanted to get to school early and find Turgid to at least say hello before the bell rang. He found himself running until he was in front of the Riverses' house. Then he slowed down to walk past the high hedges. Now he knew what those hedges hid, uncles and cousins, a random librarian, a time machine, and a mother who used to sneak out every Tuesday night hoping to become a chef. Rupert wondered if she had found a new restaurant to work in.

Even though Rupert lingered a bit in front of the hedges, there was no sign of life, so he ran on until he got to the schoolyard. Buses were unloading and the children who were driven to school were leaping out of cars; others had balls and were playing four square. There was the usual commotion on the playground and the usual gang of little toughs drifting about together looking menacing. Rupert realized he had no idea of Turgid's before-school routine, so he had no idea where to look for him and the bell rang before he could. Never mind, thought Rupert, he'd find Turgid at lunch. Surely he would be in the lunchroom.

Rupert waited impatiently all through the morning lessons. However, at lunchtime Turgid was not to be found in the lunchroom or his classroom when Rupert worked up the nerve to peek in there as well. And although he walked the perimeter of the school during lunch, Turgid wasn't outside either. Perhaps he hadn't come to school at all. Perhaps he was ill. Rupert felt a great sense of letdown but then thought, oh well, now that they were friends, they had many many school days thereafter to hang out.

However, the next day came and it was the same. Turgid was nowhere to be found. When he hadn't come all week, when Rupert realized he hadn't, in fact, seen *any* of the Riverses, he began to wonder. He had looked for Sippy in the wing of the school that housed the younger grades, but hadn't found her. He had asked Elise if she had seen her or any of the Riverses about that week.

"Sippy Rivers?" asked Elise. "Why?"

"I'm just wondering," said Rupert. "If you see her could you ask her if Turgid is sick?"

"I don't know her," said Elise, who was even shyer than Rupert.

"Well, could you ask her?" asked Rupert.

"Okay," said Elise in a small voice, but Rupert doubted she would.

Rupert's sense of letdown grew even greater. He had thought in the back of his mind that even if he didn't see Turgid, Uncle Moffat might come looking for him to finally complete their date at the Union Club or give him the six shirts that had been made for him, but he had not come by. Rupert thought that Turgid might have even told his family that it was Rupert's birthday and Mrs. Rivers might have made him a belated cake. Ever since he had done the unlikely and become friends with Turgid, ever since Turgid had told him he was like a member of the family, he thought anything was possible and had begun to entertain a whole slew of fantasies.

But now Rupert was beginning to feel that the Rivers family might not be as enamored of him as Turgid had led him to believe. On the other hand, he thought hopefully, it could be that the entire family was ill with a terrible flu and they'd all taken to their beds. Yes, he thought, that was the most likely explanation, and his adventures with them would begin anew on Monday when they were all feeling better.

But Monday came and Rupert saw neither Sippy nor Turgid at school, and no Rivers came for him with lunch plans or jewels to visit or restaurants to eat in or time machines to transport them. Rupert even found himself thinking somewhat resentfully that Mr. Rivers was the only adult in the family who apparently felt no guilt about Rupert losing all his prizes. As if, after all, he were entitled to the Riverses' atonement. He even found himself fantasizing about what form Mr. Rivers's atonement would take and hoping it involved food. But by the end of Friday when nothing new or exciting had happened, Rupert went home deflated. All week his fantasies had grown bigger and bolder until he had imagined them all begging Rupert to become some kind of family consultant, perhaps with a small salary, so had he risen in their estimation. Now he doubted anything like this would happen.

And to make matters worse, April, in the capricious way of spring, took a sudden turn from lush and warm to nasty and cold, and a gentle snow drifted down over all the budding bushes and sprouting daffodils.

Could this week get any worse?

But when he got home he realized it could, because the first thing he saw as he approached his house was his mother sitting on the sagging front steps, holding a mug of coffee between her raw red hands, and staring despairingly out into the drifting snow.

She didn't seem to notice Rupert approaching. She had snowflakes on her nose and a frozen expression.

What in the world could be up, he wondered? His mother never got home before six o'clock at night.

"Rupert!" she snapped suddenly as if coming awake. "I suppose you're wondering what I'm doing home. I suppose you are thinking I lost my job. Well, I did. But not for the reasons you probably think. Not because there was anything *wrong* with the way I cleaned. I was the best darn cleaner in that whole place, Rupert. The best darn cleaner in Steelville. I made those offices *sparkle*. And don't think I didn't!"

"Okay," said Rupert.

"I don't know what we'll do for money now. It's always been up to me. I don't know how we're going to eat. I don't know where we're going to live if we can't make the rent payments or what we're going to do. I haven't even been able to find your father to tell him yet."

This was odd too, thought Rupert. He'd never known his father to be anywhere but on the couch watching TV or in the driveway working on his Trans Am.

"And why did I lose my job? Because the steelworks is cutting back on employees and one of the cleaners had to go, they told me."

Rupert sat on a step next to his mother.

"What *will* we do?" asked Rupert anxiously. He realized that someday he might look back on these as the good old days when he got to sleep under a bed.

"We'll starve, I guess," said his mother, in her despair making no attempt to sugarcoat things. "Life isn't fair, Rupert."

Rupert's heart began beating triple fast. What *would* they do? There was little enough money for food as it was. Could he quit school and get a job? But who would hire an eleven-year-old?

"The part that really stings is that I got fired while some flibbertigibbet who only just started cleaning there two years ago got to keep her job. And why? Because *she* knows the Riverses. She's not even friends with them, but she used to deliver their newspaper so she gets to stay on. No consideration for the breadwinner of a large family. They're horrid, those Riverses. Oh, why couldn't *I* be the one who knew them? It's all about who you know in this rotten old world, Rupert. And I never knew anyone. And I'm never likely to know anyone."

"But I do!" said Rupert, leaping to his feet. "I'm *friends* with a Rivers. With all of them really. And Turgid said that if I ever needed anything I could come to him."

"Don't be stupid, Rupert," said his mother. "This is no time for make-believe."

"No, I really am. I'm friends with Aunt Hazelnut and Uncle Henry and Uncle Moffat and even Mrs. Rivers. And Turgid Rivers is my best friend."

Rupert didn't tell his mother about being blood brothers because that was a secret. But surely the blood vow was to cover just such a situation.

"Right, Rupert, I'm sure they're practically a second family to you," said his mother, snorting derisively and taking another sip of coffee as if a whole long life of listening to lies had caused her to be neither excited nor appalled by them.

"I'm not. I'm not. We can go to their house right

now and I can explain what happened—that you are my mother—and then they will give you back your job."

"Don't be silly, it wasn't a Rivers who fired me. It was the manager. I've never even met a Rivers."

"Exactly," said Rupert. "Don't you see? That's why we have to go tell them. Then they can tell the manager that he made a mistake. Come on."

Rupert stood up and yanked on his mother's sleeve, attempting to pull her to her feet.

She'd been sitting on the porch letting snow drift down on her for so long she was covered with a light dusting, as though she were a statue.

"Cut it out," said his mother. "I've had enough. All this has just knocked the stuffing out of me. Do you still have those menthol eucalyptus chips? I think this calls for polishing off the rest of them. If you want to do something for me, run along and fetch them."

Rupert went up to his bedroom to get his mother the chips from the pillow where he'd stashed them. He had planned to give them back to her anyway after a decent interval as he always did. But when he reached into the pillow and felt around, he pulled out not just the chips but the suit. *The suit!*

He raced down to the front porch, holding it out in front of him excitedly.

"Look, look!" he cried. "This is my proof. You see

this silk suit? Uncle Moffat, that's Mr. Rivers's brother, took me to the Union Club for lunch. He had this silk suit made for me. He's having six shirts made for me too, but I haven't picked them up yet! Although why he hasn't told me if they're ready, I don't know! I just keep wondering at school all day long, why doesn't he come and tell me if the shirts are ready? WHY?" Rupert was getting more and more agitated so that he had begun to rattle on, thinking out loud and sounding, he was afraid, crazy.

Mrs. Brown evidently thought so too, for she stood and backed up against the porch railing, staring at him as if he'd lost his mind.

Rupert knew that nothing he said would convince his mother, so he put the suit jacket on over his clothes and said, "Look!"

His mother looked at him in horrified silence for a moment and then put her hands over her eyes and wailed, "You shoplifted a *SUIT*? Couldn't you find something more *useful* to steal?"

"How could this have come off the rack?" he demanded. "It's been *tailored* for me."

Rupert then told her all the things he had learned about the making of the suit. The different fabrics, the weights of wool, the way it should be cut. He turned around and showed her how this suit had been put together specifically for him, and when he was done, he saw a bit of belief come into her eyes and with it a kind of massive confusion.

"But, Rupert," she said, "why would anyone give you a suit?"

"Never mind. It's a long story. But now you have to believe me so we can go to their house and tell them what happened and get your job back."

His mother stood up. She went inside and got the thin raincoat she wore all winter and put it on. He noticed that she also brushed her hair and put on lipstick. He stared at her red mouth, wondering how old the lipstick was and where she had kept it all these years, for he had never seen her wear it before. He wondered if it was the same lipstick she had worn to Coney Island that day, for her lips had been red then too.

"Well, come on," she said. "Much good it will probably do us."

As they walked to the Riverses', Rupert's heart swelled with the excitement of everything working out. Of everything leading to this happy ending, for surely once the Riverses found out his mother worked as a cleaner, they would give her a much better job.

When they got to the gate of the Riverses' house his mother turned to him and said, "How do I look?"

"You look good," said Rupert, but he knew it didn't matter how she looked because she was with *him*.

Then he pressed the buzzer on the gate. He pressed

it again. And then a third time. No one answered. He started to press it a fourth time but his mother stopped his hand.

"Don't," she said. "You don't want to make them mad. They probably have some kind of hidden camera. They can probably see who is pressing the buzzer and they don't want to answer. Well, of course they don't. Come on, let's go home. Quick, before this gets any worse."

"Maybe nobody heard," said Rupert. "They would answer if they saw it was me. And even if they were all out, they have a butler who answers the door. They even have a cook."

"A cook and a butler," said his mother breathily to herself as if the grandeur of this household were not to be believed.

Rupert rang the buzzer again and, when still no one answered, began to ring it over and over and over.

"Stop it," said his mother. "Let's split before they call the cops."

"I don't understand," said Rupert. "I'm friends with them. I really am."

"Sure, Rupert," said his mother, her old cynical tone returning. "Come on."

She pulled him from the gate and they started home, when suddenly Rupert saw the librarian coming toward them, her hands full of shopping bags.

"Hello!" he said in relief, and ran up to her.

It took her a moment to place him and then she said, "Why, it's Rupert, isn't it?"

"Yes. Mother, this is the librarian who lives with the Riverses," he said. "This is my mother, Mrs. Brown."

"How do you do, Mrs. Brown," said the librarian.

"Okay," said Rupert's mother.

"We were just coming to talk to the Riverses about something," began Rupert when the librarian interrupted.

"Oh you're too late for that," she said. "Yes, you're sadly much too late for that. They're gone."

"Gone?" echoed Rupert.

"Oh, yes. All of them."

"*All* of them? Turgid?" asked Rupert, flabbergasted.

"Yes, indeed. Mrs. Rivers moved to Cincinnati. She's opening her own diner and calling it Beth's Place. Well, you could have knocked me down with a feather. A Rivers working in a restaurant! Mr. Rivers put up a good fight, but she said she was going and taking the children with her and he could do as he pleased. Well, he was never any good without Mrs. Rivers. She was the heart and soul of *that* outfit. So off they all moved. Boom. Without a by-your-leave. I hear they're living in a hotel, looking for a house, and Mrs. Rivers is terribly happy. Now Henry, he has simply disappeared. I always did think he was a little odd. He may come back because everything he owns is still in the house, but he's been gone for days now. Before Mr. and Mrs. Rivers and the children left even. Mrs. Rivers thought the police should be informed, but Turgid said that Henry had told him he was going adventuring and not to worry if he was gone *some time*. He said there was a pun in that sentence, but I can't find it. Moffat took his children to Wisconsin to join his wife, with whom he has reunited. They are going to dairy-farm. He said they had split up because he was on the fence about it. Her ruling passion was cows. Cows! What's in a cow? he wanted to know. But eating at the Union Club reminded him, he said, that what was in a cow was steak and hamburgers, and perhaps his wife would consider having half dairy cows and half steak hamburger cows. He could get behind that. So off he popped with William, Melanie, and the other Turgid. Oh, dear, Rupert, I was supposed to tell you that your shirts are ready and you need only pick them up. I thought you might come in to the library and I'd tell you then, but you don't use the library, do you?"

"I don't have a library card," said Rupert.

"Well, you should get one. It's free, you know," said the librarian.

"Are they *really* free?" asked Rupert in astonishment. If it was true, all along there had been books for Elise. Books for him!

"Yes, Rupert, they really are," said the librarian.

"Right, free," said Mrs. Brown. "Where have I heard *that* one before?"

The librarian paid no attention, she was busy placing family members and rambled on, "Hazelnut, as you know, took off without a forwarding address. Well, they were none of them surprised about *that*—she was a Macintosh. And the cook and butler left because they had no one to cook or butler for except me and I'm not really a family member. Or, as they put it bluntly, not a prestigious-enough person to serve. It turns out that in the butlering game, it's all about *who* you work for. So it looks as if I have the house and all twenty-four bedrooms to myself. Anyhow, I'm just getting home from the grocery store. And then I've got housework to get to; the cleaning staff quit as well, or I'd ask you for tea. Were you coming over for a reason or just to visit?"

"My mother lost her job at the steelworks and we were going to ask the Riverses to make them give it back to her," said Rupert.

"I need that job," said Mrs. Brown. "Or we'll lose the roof over our heads."

"That *is* a shame," said the librarian. "I'd ask you to move in with me, but I've only twenty-four bedrooms. If I had, say, twenty-five, I'd make a guest room, but as it is, I really haven't got the space. Well, good luck to you. Best get in before the ice cream melts." And so saying, the librarian pushed the code into the security panel and the gate opened for her. She disappeared down the walkway.

Rupert stood for a second staring at the house through the gate.

"I met them and so much happened and now..." he paused, fumbling, having difficulty expressing his confusion—the time machine, Mrs. Rivers, Uncle Moffat, Aunt Hazelnut and her jewels, his friend, his *friend—poof*—all gone.

"No, I understand." His mother stared in the same direction as Rupert. "Things go by so very fast and then it's as if they never were."

His mother appeared for a second to be looking far into a past with the same expression Turgid had looking into a future he hadn't expected or wanted as she said, "It wasn't what I thought, *I* wasn't what I thought...."

Time gave you everything and took everything away again. How often could this happen to you before you didn't want to feel anything? Not the bad, not even the good?

Rupert had wanted his mother to see all that he had—the ocean, the sun dropping into the Pacific, Aunt Hazelnut's jewels, and the expressions on people's faces as they ate the sparkle salads. How lucky he had been. But maybe his mother had tired of seeing *anything*, even her own children. His father had said she was a rock. But Rupert now wondered if he was wrong. Maybe it wasn't that she had no feelings, maybe she'd just had too many of them.

As they walked home, houses on both sides of them stretched ahead like a corridor, and right at the end in the middle the sun hung, a pale wintry wonder lighting the snowy dusk. But only Rupert saw it.

When they got home they found the mail scattered on the front porch, where the mailman had thrown it. He refused to put it through the mail slot. He had a cat.

"Letter for *you*," said his mother, handing an envelope to Rupert as if nothing would amaze her anymore. She opened the front door and they went inside. "Silk suits, mail," she muttered. "The world's gone crazy." And she moved on to the kitchen, shaking her head, to begin making supper while Rupert looked at the envelope in surprise.

The only mail he'd ever gotten had been from Aunt Hazelnut, but it wasn't Aunt Hazelnut's handwriting. He ripped it open. It was from Charlie and Chas.

Dear Rupert,

We thought you would like to know how things worked out here in Florida. We can't tell Hazelnut because we don't know where she is, our letters to her have been returned, but perhaps you could pass on to her the news the next time you see or hear from her. In the meantime, we knew you'd want to know whether it was circus performers or astronauts we became. Well, we started out as one thing but then changed our minds. When we were teens Nutty used to tell me that your life was a unique and therefore glorious thing—NOBODY has one just like yours—floating about in a universe that morphs and remorphs itself and so it does, but I think she'd still be surprised to find we'd become..."

Rupert finished the sentence in amazement. He would have thought it would have been the other. He was about to reread the letter when there was a scream from the kitchen.

Everyone in the house ran there to find Mrs. Brown, oatmeal spilled all down her front, and their father standing by the stove looking pleased as punch, dressed in a suit.

"Children," said Mrs. Brown. "Your father has a job."

So then they all had to hear the story, how Mr. Brown had been working on his Trans Am in the driveway that morning when a man had stopped to ask him about it. Mr. Brown told him how he had reworked the engine and what it could do. From there they had a long chat about cars in general. The man owned a used-car lot and wanted to buy classic cars but couldn't find a mechanic he could trust to work on them. The more he and Mr. Brown talked, the more they realized they understood cars the same way—what you should and shouldn't do with them. Then the man said he wanted to not just fix up classic cars but sell them. However, he needed the right salesman. And he thought Mr. Brown was the man for him. He hired him on the spot to be both mechanic and salesman. Rupert's father would start the very next day. So that afternoon Mr. Brown had walked into town and bought a suit with the money they had saved for the next rent payment.

"A suit," whispered Rupert's mother. "Two suits in one day."

"Anyhow, don't worry, I'll get the rent payment together again. I'll be making more than you," he said to Rupert's mother in amazement.

"I always thought I'd be the one with the suit," whispered Mrs. Brown, and then told him the briefer story of losing her job.

"Hey, never mind," said Mr. Brown. "Let's not think about that until tomorrow. Let's just celebrate. Wait until you see what I got."

He dashed out to the front hall and returned with two big bags. The children clamored around him demanding to know what he had. Mr. Brown made them guess, and when they couldn't he shouted, "Hamburgers!"

Everyone ate their hamburgers huddled around the television and they were even better than Rupert had hoped. Elise, who was sitting next to him, was made bold by the happy mood in the room and jumped up.

"I got a star note today," she said. "My teacher sends them home when you've done really good work. I put it in my pillow. I'll go get it."

"Don't bother," said her mother, getting up and heading for the stairs. "You just charm those teachers. That's how you get those things. I suppose next thing you're going to be getting a suit too. I'm going to bed. I've got to look for work tomorrow."

His mother still longed for a suit and crocodile pumps and the life that went with it, thought Rupert. But it wasn't his suit that had made him happy, or any of the things the Riverses could have given him. It was what, as a result of being with them, he had seen. The Riverses were lucky to live in the very rich neighborhood. But in the very poor, the poor, the middle class, the rich, or the very rich part of town, everyone had eyes.

Aunt Hazelnut was right; your life, YOUR life, no matter who you were, no matter where you were, was a unique and glorious thing. Some lives contained more money, but all lives contained equal wonder. Although to see it you had to see everything else as well, and seeing came at the terrible price of feeling.

This is a decision you couldn't make for anyone but yourself. You could not force others to see or feel but you could share what *you* had.

"Come on," he said, jumping up and taking Elise by the hand, pulling her to her feet. They headed upstairs.

"Listen," he said, going into the bedroom, "tomorrow we're going to the library to get library cards and we'll get books of stories to read. But tonight I'll tell you one of mine."

Elise jumped into her bed and Rupert sat on the floor.

"One winter night, Elise," he began, and then the words flowed, "while all Steelville slept—the very poor, the poor, the middle class, the rich, and the very rich—I came out of a dark garage to sparkle-lit tables floating in the night...."

MANY THANKS TO:

MARIE CAMPBELL

MARGARET FERGUSON

LYNNE MISSEN

KARLA REGANOLD